Set in a near-future environment, mega-corporations have taken over the most habitable of planets, creating domed utopias for their devoted employees. Everyone else has been shunted off to a multitude of mostly habitable planets and moons where they scrape by as farmers and tradesfolk, miners and merchants, bounty hunters and scavengers.

James Marks and his crew of scav trash operate their ship, *SIO*, on a mission to obtain a mysterious piece of new tech. It changes everything and leaves him stranded somewhere he doesn't recognize with a cute, if not a bit annoying, tech scientist. James doesn't know, when he first meets Michael, but his life is about to change in a very surprising way.

SIO

C.A. Blocke

A NineStar Press Publication

Published by NineStar Press
P.O. Box 91792,
Albuquerque, New Mexico, 87199 USA.
www.ninestarpress.com

SIO

Printed in the USA
First Edition
April, 2019

Print ISBN: 978-1-950412-62-4

Also available in eBook, ISBN: 978-1-950412-48-8

Easy contracts are few and far between, 'specially out here on the outer ring. One has to learn to take any assurance that it won't be a problem to get the job done, with a grain of salt. Still, the crew's usual source of contracts was always good for the money, and they weren't exactly in a position to be choosy about what they were doing to scrape by. The simple version was heading deep into Corporate Space to obtain a piece of fresh tech from Peach Corps.

The unspoken reality was they all knew getting anything out of a Peach facility was close to a suicide run if they got caught, and they were better off paying the black-market markup for anything they were looking for. Of course, the client was looking for a prototype that wasn't exactly in the hands of anyone disreputable yet. Like most of their jobs, it was made for a small crew in a basic ship, and it didn't get much more basic than SIO.

One: The Job

"YOU'RE REALLY GOING in alone?" Edge asked, leaning heavily against the console as James plugged in the coordinates. "I thought you promised Lyra you weren't doing jobs alone anymore after that last big fuckup."

James rolled his eyes and sighed. "What Lyra don't know won't hurt her. You and your sister are wanted on every planet in Corporate Space, and I'm not about to lose the only good pilot we've got by taking Corin along for the ride. Besides, I'm fluent in bullshit. I'll be fine."

Edge laughed and drew his oversized ElectroPistol before shoving it toward James's chest. "You're gonna need this. They set up scanners every few kilometers to catch travelers with old-school bullets."

"You know I've got one." James smirked, opening his dark-brown duster to show off his special design. "And mine's overclocked."

"Show-off."

Edge and his sister, Razor, had been on the ship's crew since day one, and far too many crew members had been lost one way or another since. To be fair, James knew Edge had a point. The duster was a bit of a showpiece, but even in Corporate Space, they could appreciate fine leatherwork.

Quietly, Razor added, "Careful where you're scanning with that eye, boss. Peach detection is sensitive to all TechEyes."

James blinked several times, self-conscious at the reminder of his less-than-human status. After fifteen years on the outer ring, he was starting to feel less man than machine. An eye, a leg, and a full neural interface later, who really could say he wasn't? "Yes, mother." James sighed, offering another fond roll of the eyes. "Believe me, I'm in and out. The last place I want to hang out is a Peach Corp research and development office."

"Eye on the prize." Edge nodded, clapping a meaty hand on James's back. "Corin'll leave the engines running for ya."

GETTING IN WASN'T hard; a flash of the badge the client had provided and a few sideways glances at James's generally unkempt appearance, and he was walking the halls toward the mark's office. Thankfully, R&D didn't have half the security protocol most Corporate offices had, and as far as they cared, the dark-haired man in a duster and pressed shirt was Mr. Marquis Benton, in the flesh. However, the short middle manager staring him down didn't exactly seem convinced.

"So, Mr. Benton, is it?" he asked, stroking his fingers through professionally cropped blond hair before taking off his glasses to rub the bridge of his nose. "And you are here for?"

"I was told the communique was sent days ago," James bluffed, crossing his arms and giving the manager, Michael, a critical look. "The Rose prototype. It's being called up for Corporate preview."

"Well, as much as I'd love to have one less piece of useless technology to deal with, it's not ready. I never received this...*communique*...you're talking about."

Michael's brow furrowed as he slipped his glasses back on; the frustration apparent on his face was adorable at the very least.

"Fine. Fine." James leaned in, glancing over the man's badge to grab a name, only to feel his TechEye activate to read it through the soft fold of his worn blazer. "It's all right, Michael. I'll deal with your supervisor."

"I *am* the supervisor at this facility." Michael frowned, shaking his head. "And if that crappy old TechEye wasn't such a piece of outdated *shit* running firmware from ten years ago, you would have been able to pull up my personnel file and would know that."

It wasn't quite the same as being caught red-handed, and security wasn't swarming the office yet, so there was that much hope. "Hey, you know how crappy the pay is for runners. I haven't exactly been able to keep up on the latest and greatest." James shrugged, and then stepped closer, ready to make a move, if justified. "Besides, I don't like all that clutter in my HUD. All I need is to get this prototype to my boss." It was a fair enough statement; the heads-up display on the older chip software was much less cluttered with information of various levels of situational importance. In the long run, it made it difficult to parse the large amount of information that wasn't actually in front of his eyes but tended to render him at least distracted when it came up.

Michael stood, one hand on his black leather belt and the other casually planted against his desk. "The new heads-up display is actually quite streamlined by comparison, especially if you have the visual upgrade." He shifted on his feet and, after a moment's pause, dropped his gaze down to the litter of papers and scraps on his desk. "Look, okay... I don't know who you are or how you got in here, but contrary to popular belief, just because I'm in R&D, I'm not a fucking idiot. The Rose is classified, and you've done absolutely nothing to make me believe you should even be here."

James had been in worse situations, which really said quite a lot about his chosen profession. He put on his best smile and leaned across Michael's desk, drawing eyes back up to him. "I'll level with you, Michael. There was no communique, okay? I know I'm sort of jumping the gun here, but bringing back the Rose and blowing the bigwigs' minds with it pretty much guarantees a promotion that...uh...well, I need. And I know you've got zero reason to believe a word I'm saying, but I can definitely put in a good word for the new *head* of R&D."

Michael's eyes narrowed behind his thin spectacles, and James felt his heart rate raise enough to hear the blood pounding in his ears. Lying was no big thing, but pulling shit in a Peach facility was a damn bold move for someone not looking to end up in a prison colony for the rest of their short, crappy life. Finally, Michael said, "Head of R&D? You have that kind of power? I thought you said you were a runner."

"A runner for someone with more power than both of us combined. With the right offering, I could do quite a lot"—James whispered, licking his lower lip for dramatic effect, if not sheer nerves—"with a little help from a certain smart and handsome developer."

A long moment passed, and James realized exactly how that statement had come off. Fortunately, Michael seemed to buy it, and James wasn't really lying—for everything his bookish appearance gave off, Michael was handsome in a sort of cute tech-nerd kind of way. Michael sighed and shook his head, drawing back. "You've got a silver tongue, Marquis. And, I guess I'm just sick of looking at the stupid thing," he muttered under his breath, heading toward the door James had come in. "I have to get it from the lab; they're working on it today."

"Of course, of course." James feigned a laugh while following him back into the corridor and through the honeycomb of hallways and nondescript rooms toward the lab.

Michael scanned his card and then turned back to face him. "Wait here."

There was a delicate dance—James couldn't wait too long out in the open without being checked by security, who would likely figure out his papers were fake, within a few seconds, but he also had to offer Michael the benefit of the doubt, lest his true intention be made even clearer. He nodded and casually folded his arms over his chest, gently patting the pistol concealed within his coat. Beyond the door, he couldn't see much more than several bodies in white suits with blank faces moving quietly around, and then he was alone in the corridor.

Ten minutes and one close call with security passed, and James couldn't stop himself from attempting to listen at the door, to no avail. Daring the chance of getting caught, he fumbled out the jack in his coat pocket, connecting it to the keypad first and then directly to the port behind his left ear. Hacking was dangerous in the best possible circumstances. Getting caught was almost a certainty, but the cybernetic jack made it a little simpler to do something as innocuous as jimmying a lock—hell, James had practically grown up forcing locks with or without technological assistance. Unfortunately, Razor wasn't wrong about Peach Corp being on top of outside tech in their systems. The lock gave, after only a few moments of forcing the code, the door opened, and the first thing James saw after pulling the jack free at both ends in one yank was security coming right for him.

"What are you doing in here?" Michael shouted as James rushed into the room, slamming the door behind him. A steel case was open on a large table, a small purple rose made of circuits and glass seated in a holding point fixed inside the case.

"Okay, so here's the thing..." James stammered, letting the words come as his most useful form of self-preservation. "There are at least three guys with ElectroPistols on the other side of that door, and I really need to leave with this prototype, so if you could close that case, I'll be heading out now."

"It's not ready!" Michael answered, lifting the safety goggles from around his glasses and tossing them on the floor with an angry sigh. "Do you even know *anything* about the Rose? You have got to be the most *ignorant—*"

James cut him off for lack of time more than anything, snapping the case closed. "I may have to use you as a human shield...no worries; ElectroPistols don't hurt nearly as bad as the real thing." He was well aware it sounded bad, but to the best of his knowledge, as long as the person being shot didn't have too many cybernetic parts, the blasts weren't usually deadly. James grabbed Michael's elbow, thankful he was a little lighter and a good deal shorter than most.

They made it two steps to the door, and when James touched the latch, a loud popping noise was accompanied by a rush of heat, and everything went black.

Two: Strange Land

IT WAS HOT. As he slowly came to, that was the first impression of what James would later find out was the outer rim planet of Terro 9. His body buzzed with electric current, a small jolt piercing behind his ear with a high-pitched humming noise.

"You know, for someone who was able to get into a secure facility, you're an idiot." Michael's clipped voice came from right beside James. He tried to open his eyes and saw only blinding light. "Don't open them yet. The circuits on your TechEye shorted out. I'm working on it."

"Wha—" James managed to move his lips only to feel another pulse of electricity. "Careful there! That's my eye you're poking."

"No, it's your implant I'm poking. And I'm not poking; I'm performing a subsurface-level diagnostic. We've never used the Rose with someone who has implants."

"Sight would be nice. I mean, unless this is some prison ring of hell security has dragged me to."

"You, my dear fucking idiot, are nowhere near security. Or Peach Corps. Or even Corporate Space." Another buzzing zap sent a flash of light to James's brain, giving the brief impression of shadows and a blazing sun. "You are, without a doubt, the *worst* Corporate spy I've ever met—and believe me, I've met a lot of them. They would have known you don't fuck with a prototype. I mean, if you even had half a brain, you would at least have the intel to know that we've been working on a teleportation device. An attractive but currently useless teleportation device. Said device creates a halo of energy that, when combined with any other current—in this case, latent static electricity—sends the holder *somewhere* in the universe. But hey, consider yourself lucky we actually landed on a planet or moon or something and didn't get shot into space like the last idiot who tried to steal it."

James let Michael continue with whatever he was doing, content for a minute to allow everything he was saying to sink in. And hey, at least it could be worse. "Well, we aren't dead."

"Oh goody, an optimist. I'd add that we aren't dead *yet*," Michael muttered under his breath. "Count backward from fifty. I assume you can count."

Rather than give him the satisfaction of answering, James started counting down, the numbers seeming to summon a loud click and *whirr* followed by flashing of his HUD with information flickering fast and garbled. "What the hell did you do? Stop that!"

"It's a minor upgrade; let it run. Whoever did your initial install was a hack."

"Well *excuse me*, not all of us have access to the best code monkeys in the galaxy," James grumbled. "And for the record, I'm not a Corporate spy, okay? It was nothing personal. Just a job."

"Oh, even better—a merc. I'm stuck on some desolate planet with a fucking merc."

Blinking, James managed his eyes open as the HUD closed, looking up at the endless blue sky above them before catching the brightness of the sun and then looking to Michael. "Do you ever calm down? I mean, yeah, it's hot and we don't really know where we are, but it could be a whole lot worse."

"Calm down. Right. I'll tell you when I feel like I'm *calm*, given that you've basically kidnapped me." Michael frowned deeply and folded the small pouch of tools he'd been using, into his blazer pocket. "I hope you're scanning right now."

"Sure. Right. On it." James blinked again and then rubbed his eyes before focusing on the other man, pulling up his ident card and personnel file to find, apparently, Michael really did upgrade the software. "Michael Bennet. Unmarried, no children. Wow. You have worked for Peach for a *very* long time."

"Not me, idiot. The horizon, the sky, the ground, fucking soil samples! Anything to figure out how far out we are."

Michael had a point, but James wasn't exactly in the mood for it, given he was probably quite far away from his ship, and his crew were undoubtedly getting antsy about why he wasn't back with the score yet. With a sigh, James set to work gathering what information he could. It all lead back to a singular "unknown." "It's not in my memory. I got nothing, well...it's hot. And has two suns, probably a really long day cycle. And there seems to be some kind of civilization about six kilometers south."

Michael grunted. "Fine. It's a good place to start." He pushed up out of the hard-packed sand, gathering himself but not offering James a hand up. Without looking back, Michael started heading out toward the east.

"Uh, I know I'm apparently an idiot, but south is over there." James pointed out the right direction, pushing up with a frustrated groan. He tried to pick himself back up, only to realize too late his right leg wasn't moving with him. "Ah, fuck..." He braced himself as he stumbled forward, hitting the hard sand face-first. "So, uh...little problem here."

Michael swore under his breath, turning back toward James to catch him, grunting and rolling until James was splayed out, peering back at Michael with a sheepish smile. "You have a mechanical leg, don't you?"

"I prefer the term 'artificial limb analogue'; thank you very much."

"Hydraulic would have suited you better. Those damn cybernetics are touchy when you take on a large amount of current." He frowned, furrowed his brow, and then jogged over to sink to his knees beside James again, withdrawing his tools.

"Yeah, but mine's interesting. And in my defense, I don't exactly get electrocuted on a daily basis."

Michael shrugged. "Fair enough." A long, awkward moment passed before James realized Michael was waiting for him.

"Oh, pants off?"

"Unfortunately."

James tried to toe off his boots, managing the easy one before nudging at his dead leg with his foot. "Little help here?"

Michael swore again, the corners of his mouth twitching like he might smile, though it didn't come. "You know, I never really thought the next time I took a guy's pants off it would be in the middle of nowhere."

"One of the perks of being a *fucking merc*. Travel to distant and exotic lands...have total strangers take your pants off."

"Shut up or I'm not fixing it."

"Just saying…" James lifted his hips, helping with the process of getting off his boot and trousers as best he could. "This really is a lot more fun with control of all my limbs."

"Says you." Michael chuckled, neatly folding James's worn denim pants before setting them aside. "I think I prefer you not moving."

"Funny! So you do have a sense of humor lurking in there." James glanced down at him, feeling the familiar tug of flirty banter warming him. "Thing is, there's much easier ways to render me immobile without the whole getting stuck in the middle of nowhere with a fried servo thing."

Ignoring James's implication, somewhat shockingly, given how often it usually worked for James, Michael answered, "I'm pretty sure the servos are okay, but I won't know until I open you up."

"Hey, hey, hey! At least buy a guy a drink first!" James laughed, clearly a little nervous when he heard the plink and scrape of a tiny screwdriver behind his knee.

Michael was quiet as he went to work taking off the limited knee plating and showing it to James like some goddamn tech sadist. James dozed lightly, thanks to the blazing hot suns, but after a long while, he felt Michael's fingers gently stroking along his thigh where metal met skin. It was a sensation he hadn't felt in a long time, the tiny tingle of skin exploring skin. Michael asked, "How did it happen?"

"Hmm?" James pushed himself up on his elbows, to catch Michael's attention focused down at the old jagged scarring and darkened flesh. The tip of Michael's tongue was visible against his lower lip, as was the hand with a compact ElectroDriver poised on a screw half tightened down. James shifted his pelvis in an attempt to ward off the tender, curious touch, but it only made Michael's fingers trace the seam more intently. "Sack of gold and a tinkerer willing to work off the books."

"You know that's not what I meant." A single finger slid up and traced over a jagged claw mark several inches above the tear in James's flesh. "This wasn't just an upgrade."

"Ohhkay…" James groaned and bit down on his lower lip to hold back the fact that Michael's touch was almost too intimate to handle, given the circumstances. "Had a run-in on a job. Turns out you don't fuck with people who keep killbeasts for pets."

Michael made a sound in the back of his throat that seemed sad, but James wasn't about to ask if it meant he'd keep the gentle touches going. Thankfully, his hand backed away and he patted James's metal leg gently. "All right, powering you up. This will probably hurt."

None of James's non-fleshy features had been hard-booted since they were installed, and he learned the hard way that 'probably hurt' wasn't even close to an adequate description. In this instance, it was a little closer to being fully numb from the waist down on both sides and then submerged in boiling water. James cried out, only to have Michael throw himself over his torso to cover James's mouth with his hand. "Shh, we have no idea what's out here. Unless you like the idea of meeting another killbeast, I'd keep it down."

Gritting his teeth, James rode out the wash of pain long enough to calm himself before Michael pulled away his hand. "Again…drinks first, okay?"

Michael frowned. "I'm pretty sure I hate you."

"They usually do." James flexed his legs, feeling the pressure down through his thigh for the first time in years, and then his leg bent and allowed the act of movement. "At first."

"Come on." Michael huffed, scrambling off James with a diminished glower. "We've got a lot of sand between here and somewhere that will probably kill us."

THE WALK WAS silent save for Michael's occasional reminders to keep scanning for anything in the memory files of James's neural interface and more-than-occasional complaints about how hot it was. By the time the small town was in sight, both their jackets had migrated to flopping limply over one shoulder, shirts open to provide some potential for relief to their sweat-soaked torsos.

Calling the place a town was romanticizing the fact it was mostly a few street vendors, a bar, and what might be a place to catch their bearings in the middle of a series of shacks and small houses. Basically, it could have passed for where James grew up.

"Let me do the talking." James took point as they walked through town to little notice. "They aren't exactly fans of the overeducated Corporate type out here on the ring."

Michael shot him a furrowed brow that faded to a resigned look and tucked his tools and badge deeper into his pants pocket.

One hotel was usually same as the next in the worker towns. Clean enough mercs and scavs passing through might stop for a good night's rest before taking off again, but likely to outright terrify someone who wasn't used to seeing whores in broad daylight and a filthy wooden bar. Walking through the doors, James tossed his duster into Michael's arms and made a point of letting the weapon on his hip be seen. Dominance, a declaration if anyone wanted to fuck with James Marks, he was ready to play. The sleepy smattering of clientele didn't seem to notice, in favor of crowding around a holoscreen playing a cycled dance routine of a blue-skinned woman doing a half-assed striptease.

"Looks like you landed pretty far out, traveler." A weatherworn sack of leather dressed like a man slouched onto the business side of the bar. "Need a drink?"

"Water'll do," James answered, adding, "You take credits, right?"

The bartender laughed, a raspy low sound that made them both wince inwardly. "You don't look like no Corpy. Your manservant, maybe...but you've been around. You got gold."

Michael looked up at James with a startled, pleading glance behind his spectacles. James was familiar with near panic when he saw it, and Michael already looked about to break.

"Man, my piece-of-shit ship crapped out on me before I made it to the exchange after a job, okay? Just waiting on my crew to fix it, but I figured if I've got a night to sleep in a different bed, I'm gonna take it."

Looking them over, considering the story, the barman made a guttural groan. "If it's good, you can stay. Fifty credits room and meal. Water's extra. Companionship's extra."

"A room and something drinkable will do, friend." James smiled, glad to see something working after the most recent string of suck. He held out a hand to Michael for his card, and rolled his eyes when Michael didn't understand what he was asking for, after a long moment. "Card. Please." James looked back to the host with an exasperated sigh. "Hard to find good help. Bought this one off one of those caravans around Tibur a few months back, and he's been nothing but trouble."

"Tibur's no good for slaves. Wives, maybe, but they're all too soft like your boy."

Michael recovered quickly enough, but not without a scowl as James handed over the card and watched the host run it through a dusty scanner and returned it with a sufficiently satisfied look.

"Mishca, guests! Water!" he called toward a lovely young woman with unexpectedly pale skin, light hair, and almond eyes who skittered out from the back carrying a large sealed container of water and an oversized ring full of keys.

"Come," she said simply, gesturing for them to follow.

They followed her up two flights of stairs to the end of a long hallway to a room that was frankly less than expected for the price. But, it had a comfortable-looking bed and was out of the sun, so it served their purpose.

Michael took the water, paced to the bed, and sank down with a sigh when the door slammed closed behind the servant. "You realize they've probably already tracked my card, right? They'll know where you are."

"And by the time they make it out this far, we'll be long gone. 'Less you see yourself waiting here for Peach to catch up to you."

Michael tossed aside their coats before cracking open the top and taking a long drink off the glass bottle. Casting his eyes downward, he shook his head. "That's not a good idea. Do you have a plan?"

James noted the caution in Michael's words. He didn't have the heart to say he was pretty much winging it. "I have a few ideas." He shrugged and sank into the bed with a sigh of pleasure at the soft ticking under his back. "First, we get some rest and a meal. I didn't exactly expect today to be such an adventure."

Michael sighed. "I'm your slave now, really?"

"Hey, indentured servitude is alive and well on the outer planets, man. It was the easiest way to pass you off as anything but exactly what you are."

"I'd say something witty, but I'm too tired to care."

"Look..." James turned his head to watch Michael lean back against the wall the bed butted up against, taking the opportunity for a lingering and appreciative look "Can we just agree that I was doing my job, you were doing your job, and things got kind of fucked up?"

"Yeah, by you." Michael took another drink and passed the jug over before crossing his arms over his chest.

"Well, it's not like I woke up this morning figuring I'd be ruining someone's life, okay?" James gave him a frustrated look that saw Michael break into a mild smile. "See, logic. You don't hate me."

"Yeah, I kind of do. But no, you didn't ruin my life," Michael said softly.

A loud knock at the door caught their attention, and James opened it to the servant pressing a pot and a hard loaf of bread into his arms. "One moment, Miss...?" he asked, flashing a sympathetic smile. "Is there a city on this rock? I'm looking for some specialized equipment."

She looked down before she answered, clearly trained not to speak much to the clientele. "Aurora is the biggest city, but it is a day's travel on the train... Walking would not be advisable."

"Perfect. When does the train stop here?" James walked away, offering her space as much as he was handing the bread to Michael and setting down the hot pot.

"At the dawn of the first sun," she answered. "It stops only long enough to get fuel before moving on to Craggy Point and Storm's Eye, then stops at second dusk in Aurora proper."

James nodded and dug into his pocket to withdraw one of the few small gold coins he'd managed to hold on to. "Thank you." He pressed the coin into her hand and watched with a small smirk as she hurriedly tucked it into her apron and excused herself.

"So, a train?" Michael asked once the door had closed. He opened the lid of the pot and stared into the murky brown stew with obvious pessimism. "I take it this somehow plays into your vague idea of rescuing us?"

"Are you always such an asshole, or is it because of the whole 'accidentally going on an adventure' thing?" James settled down beside him, tore a large chunk off the dry loaf of bread, and dipped it into the foreign stew.

Michael frowned again, his face lined with exhaustion and worry as he forced himself to take a hesitant bite.

"Come on," James said. "Think of it this way: you get to go on an adventure with space outlaw extraordinaire James Marks, and when it's all over you'll get to go home safe and sound while I'm probably going to end up dead or in a prison colony."

Michael shrugged and took several more bites before answering. "We'll see how it works out. Do I even want to know what animal this is?"

"Probably not." It was tough, chewy, but ultimately delicious, considering James had been living on protein bars and liquid supplements for at least two weeks.

They ate in silence with nothing really left to say. As the suns set, Michael resigned himself to stripping off his shirt and curling up on the bed.

"Hey, two to a bed..." James laughed, shouldering off his open shirt to join him. Pressed belly to belly, it was actually quite comfortable, if not a little awkward. "You gotta admit this isn't too bad."

"I could be at home in my nice bed full of familiar food watching a telenovela right now."

"And I could be on my ship counting my take of fifty thousand gold. But hey, at least we aren't alone."

"Yeah...I guess." Michael rolled onto his back, stretching his arms above his head. The sight of a long vertical scar down Michael's left arm brought more questions about the stranger.

"Office accident?" James asked, reaching out to grasp Michael's forearm, his thumb pressed down gently against the old scar.

Michael yanked his arm away and rolled his back toward his bedmate. "None of your business, James."

Three: The Train

THEY HEARD THE train shortly before dawn and felt the rumbling vibration of something heavy moving much faster than anticipated toward the little town. James built a fire in the small pit in the middle of the room, heating up a pot of wash water before Michael woke to give them both the simple pleasure of cleaning up as best they could before heading out. Michael's scar lingered in James's mind, his imagination figuring where it might have come from, but the fact that Michael was actually adjusting much better than someone in his position really should outright bothered him. They washed in quiet compromise—well...Michael compromised to listening to James hum, at least—and they left the empty bar well before the first sun rose.

"Have you ever ridden a train before?" James asked as they walked toward the shaded outcropping where leathery men were smoking stinking black stubs as they waited to load up barrels of fuel.

Michael shook his head. The modern trains were a miracle in their day, faster than anything running on steam or coal or fossil fuels, but they had lost favor over the years everywhere but the most backwoods of the outer ring once the Corporations started pumping out electric vehicles that ran on everything from solar to fusion power. It was pretty obvious that this one was practically a dinosaur by Peach Corp standards, huge and pumping out the purple smoke of a silicone-based fuel.

Pulling into the makeshift station, the lengthy train let out tendrils of purple-white smoke they followed down the shining rounded cars at a quick clip. James pulled Michael along, each step propelled a little longer until they were running, scanning for a car that was mostly full and probably wouldn't take on more cargo before reaching Aurora.

"Is this even legal?" Michael shouted as they skittered to a stop, sliding in the loose sand along the track as James located what he was looking for. Digging into his duster, he found his jack and plugged in, hooking it to the keypad on the sliding door. "I guess that answers my question."

"On this adventure..." James muttered, trying to focus more on forcing the lock than conversation. Numbers and letters whirred across James's higher brain functions, finding the right combination to open the train door. "Let's just say the odds of living are higher if you don't think too much about the law."

"Close your eyes," Michael said sharply. James heard the scrape of plastic from Michael's tool pouch and closed his eyes right as he felt the zap behind his ear. "A pulse of current will increase the output through the jack."

James really didn't need to know why; all he needed was the successful whir of the door sliding open. "You're good at this." James grinned, leaving the jack in his port as he grasped both sides of the door and pulled himself up into the train car. The hollow hiss of the brake spurred him into action, and he reached out to offer a hand up. "Come on, we don't have a lot of time."

Michael made it into the car as the train jolted and whistled for the workers to clear the track. "I always figured trains were more comfortable, you know, with seats..."

James shrugged and then muscled the door closed by throwing his weight toward the handle. Instead of a cozy self-contained travel car, they'd found their way into one full of barrels and boxes with enough squeeze space to try to get comfortable.

Michael sighed and then looked up at James before sinking down against the solid metal wall with his legs outstretched. "What now?"

"Not much. I'd try to jack into the train's communications array and contact my ship, but the chances of being caught are pretty much a given."

"And let me guess: this is the kind of illegal where we could get shot if we do get caught." Michael closed his eyes, leaning back against the wall.

"Probably just thrown off the train at high speed. Wouldn't want to risk harming the cargo." Michael's sigh, in response to the thought, prompted James to reach out, patting his shoulder as he sat down beside him. "We're not going to get caught. I've done this on way more dangerous planets." It was true enough; James had done a few train jobs that could have easily gone south and occasionally did. Their execution was nothing big, just hitching a ride.

The train rumbled below them, pulling away from the platform, and then quickly accelerated to the full speed of a modern bullet train as it cut through the desert with little to no notice from the local population.

"Right, because that's a much easier threat of death to swallow," Michael muttered under his breath. "Don't worry, the outlaw says, everything will be fine."

James shook his head. "Look, I'm not gonna say everything will be *fine* because it probably won't be. I mean, we're both in unfamiliar territory. Who knows how far away my ship is, and I can't even communicate with them until tonight, assuming we can find a safe place to hide wherever we're on our way to. All I can tell you is I'm doing everything I can to make sure *you* get out of this alive because I know this is my fault. All right?"

Michael opened his mouth like he was about to say something and then closed it again. He looked toward the door with a resigned sigh. Sure, there weren't too many ways to come back from that sort of thing, but it was the truth. James had never intended to get anyone into anything they might not get out of, and whether he knew it or not, the odds of him getting away with the heist gone wrong were increasingly slim.

They dozed off and on in the early morning cool, the heat of the day rousing James to find Michael once more with his tinkering tools, taking them to the chip James had stored in his duster's inner pocket. "That's mine," James said, looking sidelong at him. "You could have asked instead of rifling through my pockets."

"I was bored, and your snoring was louder than the train." Michael answered simply, using his thumb to roll the small chip over in his palm. "This looks like a Peach chip...seven or eight years old, but I know this design."

"The guy I got it from said it would enable me to interact with my HUD visually and make life a little easier."

"Not just you," Michael added, shifting on the metal floor to turn toward James. "It creates a holographic tablet from your HUD that gives anyone who can see it direct access to your cybernetic capabilities. When they were released, they were thought to be indispensable, but there were a few bugs in the code."

"If you call a complete lack of security, occasional malfunctions, and splitting headaches bugs in the code."

James reached out and snatched it away to store it once more in the inner pocket.

"The revisions were much more stable. Did he happen to tell you which version it is?"

James chuckled dryly as he grabbed for the bottle of water they'd brought to slake his thirst before answering. "No, unfortunately, he had a nasty bout of homicide when the bounty hunter tracking him was able to access the chip remotely and enact the kill protocol."

"K-kill protocol?" The color drained from Michael's face, and for a moment, James felt sorry for him. He couldn't guess what it was like to live in a world where his life revolved around safety and comfort, to not know a life of tech-savvy bounty hunters who could simply turn you off if you had too many enhancements.

"Yeah, seems us outworlders have a pretty good reason to fear technology and living in a world where a line of code could fry your brain." James looked away, unable to watch Michael as he lay out on the floor and curled into the fetal position. "Story is, it was a bug and Peach got rid of it years ago, but this old tech is pretty new out here. I held on to it for emergencies, and I guess to sort of remember that no matter how helpful it is, tech is dangerous."

"Just...stop talking," Michael muttered. "I don't want to talk about this."

"Suit yourself." James shrugged, glancing over to see only Michael's back and the arm of his spectacles pushed high up on his head. "We've got a lot of time to kill."

THEY DIDN'T SPEAK again until after the first stop. James left Michael in the train car to gather his thoughts and took the limited time they had before departure to put his old skills to use. It really was amazing what a silver tongue and quick fingers could do when someone was desperate. Coming back with a small pack loaded down with food and water, not to mention the additional pouch of gold tucked into his duster, James found his new companion curled up on the floor, apparently staring at nothing.

"Glad to see you're still alive," James said quietly, settling back in beside him. "Any trouble while I was away?"

The train whistled, the piercing sound cutting through the low din of daily life in the town. "No," Michael answered, rolling onto his back. "You?"

"I have supplies and the same number of holes in me as when I left. I think it's a success." Michael tore into the pack before James could finish his thought, digging out a neatly wrapped protein bar and a fresh bottle of water. "You're welcome."

"What is this?" he asked, unwrapping the bar and staring at it. "Some kind of bread?"

James couldn't hold back a laugh. It'd figure that Corporate Space wouldn't have to know what they were. "Protein bar. Created to feed the prison colonies and mining operations. They contain a full day's worth of protein, fat, vitamins, and everything else you need to get through the day without all that pesky flavor to get in the way."

Michael grimaced as he took a bite, then chewed slowly with a marked frown. "I miss the questionable stew from last night."

James shrugged, holding his meal off a little longer. "Eh, you get used to them. They're cheap and keep practically forever."

Michael nodded and managed to finish his bar as James rested his eyes, letting his body once more acclimate to the steady pulse of the train heading toward the next destination. After a while, he said, "I'm sorry. About the chip, you know... I didn't realize."

James opened his eyes again, considering the apology for what it sounded like—guilt. "You didn't kill anyone. Peach did." He shrugged. "And even if he didn't have the tech, that bounty hunter would have killed him eventually, anyway. Just the way it is out here."

Michael took the cap off his water and sipped, looking once more to the closed door as he spoke. "I designed that chip."

A hollow thud of desert detritus banged against the side of the car in the moment of dumbfounded silence that came over James. He didn't know why the thought hit him as hard as it did, but in the moment, James couldn't think of anything better to say, so he said, "No. I mean, there must have been a dozen office drones working on a project like that."

Michael looked up at him then, wetness already glossing over his eyes, and James's gut sank again. "No," Michael said. "It was one of my first big solo projects, revolutionary for the time, something to replace every device used for education, work, and entertainment. Something every man, woman, and child would demand." He looked down, staring into the bottle of water on the floor between them. "The first time they told me they wanted a shutdown protocol, I—I—" he stammered and heaved a deep sigh. "I thought they meant something that would fry the chip, make it totally useless. As it so happens after the first alpha test, they...uh...they made it clear it wasn't for shutting down the device."

"So wait; let me get this straight. *You wrote the fucking kill script*?" James shouted, staring down at Michael, his hands clenched into shaking fists. He'd seen some fucked-up shit, done some fucked-up shit even, but the thought of wiring every man, woman, and child to die with a few keystrokes was pure evil.

"No!" Michael looked up, jaw set firmly. "I didn't write the fucking script, okay? I-I went back to my office and I tried to quit. Do you know what they do to people who quit, *James*?" He hissed between clenched teeth, "Because I didn't. I didn't know until I was offered the option of my mother's life for writing it."

"Michael..." James started, watching as Michael's eyes flashed dark and he yanked up his sleeve. The cuff button popped off as the fabric was pulled to, once more, show James the scar he'd been curious about the night before.

"I opted out. Well, I mean... I tried to opt out. Obviously that didn't go very well, seeing as how I'm here." His eyes glared down at the old scar. "I was young and stupid. They found me, checked me into a medical facility, and kept me there for almost two years. I guess, when I got out, I was a more well-adjusted man because they gave me a promotion and my own apartment in the office complex." He laughed a little bitterly. "This is actually the first time I've left the complex in I don't know...five, six years?"

When Michael looked back up at him, James understood. Michael wasn't the man he'd made him for: another simple tech guy with no life. He was a broken man, a casualty of the Corporation system. For a second, James felt sorry for him and then just felt for him. James reached out and started with an arm around Michael's shoulders and ended with warm lips kissing. Michael froze under his unexpected touch, after a long moment, allowing James the comfort of stroking through his short-cropped hair, before pulling away.

"That was kind of an inappropriate response," Michael said stiffly. "I mean, usually you don't kiss people after they admit to attempted suicide almost a decade ago."

James swallowed hard, forcing a weak smile. "I tend to do that when I don't really know what to say," he admitted, lowering his head before adding, "and I've kind of wanted to do that since last night." It wasn't a lie. Michael was handsome, sure, but more importantly, very good with his tools, and James really did admire that in a person he was attracted to.

"Oh," Michael said, looking away again.

James had hoped he would say something—a hurtful remark, a pointed barb, anything but the silence that only made the whirr of the train sound louder. After several long minutes, James asked, "Was it at least an all-right kiss? I mean, it took your mind off the past, right?"

Michael's shoulders slumped, and James waited for the backlash. Instead, he laughed. It was a soft sound at first, barely a chuckle, and then Michael leaned back and looked at James with ruddy cheeks and shining eyes and laughed until James was laughing with him out of sheer confusion. Unexpectedly, Michael reached out and grabbed James by the collar of his shirt and pulled him close, kissing his jaw and then his cheek before finally finding his lips and sealing them with comfortable warmth. Then, the moment was over, and he reclined back against the metal wall and laughed again, pink tongue darting over his lips. "Yeah," Michael said. "I guess I kind of thought about it too."

"Right...so this is what we're doing, then? Kissing on a train in the middle of nowhere?" James grinned again, shaking his head at the oddity of it.

"I'm not tired enough to sleep any longer."

It wasn't much, but James took Michael's languid smile for the awkward flag it was and let it draw him in. Allowing himself to relax, he scooted closer and leaned in to kiss Michael again. His fingers hesitated on the arms of Michael's glasses until he whispered agreement, and then again he paused until Michael closed the distance between him to encourage the much-needed affection.

Four: Aurora

THE SECOND STOP was a blur of heat-tired kisses giving way to picking through the boxes of useless ore, and then a long afternoon nap that didn't end until the first sun dipped below the horizon, chased by the second to create an orange haze over the platform they jumped off on. Helping Michael down, James looped an arm around his shoulders, and they disappeared into the bustle of foot traffic. Things had changed, something had clicked, and for the moment, it worked.

Aurora was a far cry from the huge cities on other planets, not only in Corporate Space but out on the rim as well; still, it proved to be a metropolis compared to what they'd seen of the planet so far. The occasional neon signs and oil lamps lit the dusty main drag of town and a few major throughways, proclaiming everything from cheap food to escorts to tech.

"Look." Michael leaned into James's arm, pointing toward a dusty billboard that read 'Best Beds on Terro 9.' "Terro 9—is that where we are?"

James stopped in his tracks, accessing his memory databanks, digging for any mention of Terro 9 and Aurora. Thankfully, they all lit up. "Yeah, I've got coordinates. Nice." He grinned, squeezing Michael against his side with a half laugh. "Now, time to find a place to crash for the night."

"Yeah, well if you're planning on using my—"

James cut him off. "No need, my worrisome one. It's taken care of." Leading him down an alley, James found a place that looked like it would have exactly what they needed and guided him through the door. Michael stayed quiet, apparently ready for another round of impressing the locals as James swept through the bar toward the counter. "Would I be correct in assuming you have a reputable data uplink here?" He flashed a broad smile when a plain-looking man with shaggy hair and a gaunt leanness to him turned toward them. "With room fee, of course. I've no ill intention in your fine city."

"Yeah, all right," the man responded with a nod. "Room comes with basic uplink, microbial shower, and transport pass if you got a ship with you."

"Just waiting for one, actually. Should be here tomorrow or the next, but that sounds like a fantastic bargain, wouldn't you agree, darling?" James looked to Michael with a wicked smirk, only to be met with wide, shocked eyes. "Don't mind him, he's a little shy around strangers since we left Corporate Space... You know, seeing the galaxy and all."

The stranger half laughed under his breath and slid a datapad across the smooth countertop. "Don't care. Twenty gold and a thumbprint."

James swallowed hard, in silent prayer to any potential gods that might be listening that his prints hadn't already ended up in the police databases. He tossed the thin gold strips down and pressed a thumb on the warm screen. They watched, holding their breath, as his name flashed across the screen, followed by a glowing yellow THREAT LEVEL MODERATE.

"Eh, good enough." The stranger shrugged. "Stay outta trouble, and don't break m'stuff, or I'll have to call in the authorities, understood?"

"Yes, of course!" Michael piped up unexpectedly, a thin arm wrapping around James's waist. "No trouble here, just enjoying our vacation. Right, uh...honey?"

"Darling..." James muttered, shaking his head as he leaned down and pressed a kiss on Michael's forehead. "We appreciate your discretion, sir. If we require an additional night, I'll be sure to bring down the fee."

THEY BARELY MADE it through the door before collapsing to the floor in a fit of laughter. For his part, James couldn't believe the gusto Michael gave selling the routine as though it would even be questioned for a second. "The look—" James hiccupped, holding his gut. "—the look on your face when you called me honey! Fucking priceless. I can't believe you!"

"Hey!" Michael giggled, lifting his glasses to rub his eyes. "It worked, didn't it? No awkward questions."

"No, no...you're right. There was nothing at all awkward about that. Not one bit." James snorted, unable to keep a straight face. "Of course, you realize this means I absolutely *must* sleep with you now. I'd be disappointed if I didn't have off with a man who called me *honey* with such a constipated look on his face."

"You're terrible!" Michael retorted, punching James weakly in the shoulder. "I really do hate you; you know that, right?"

"Of course. Most people do." James grinned even wider, leaning in close. "At least until they fall madly in love with me."

Michael rolled his eyes. "Certainly *mad*."

Closing the distance between them, James brushed a somewhat hesitant kiss to Michael's lips, a little surprised when he returned it with the same softness as before. Michael's hands slid under James's duster, a thumb brushing against a shirt button before sliding comfortably to his back. "You know..." James murmured, kissing him again. "There is a very nice bed waiting for us to break it in."

Michael choked, a flush warming his skin as he leaned back to look James in the eyes. "You are incorrigible; you know that?"

"I have no idea what that means, but it probably fits," James answered, shrugging off his coat before plucking open his shirt buttons. "I'm fine with starting right here."

"It means the bed is fine..." Michael answered, turning away from James as he pushed back up on his feet. "I haven't done this in way too long."

"What, men, or a good old swapping fluids?"

"Ugh, you are such a—"

"What?" James cut him off, dropping his shirt to the floor. "Jackass? Outlander? Scav? Piece of anti-Corporate shit?"

When Michael turned back, he was grinning, fingers paused halfway down his once-white shirt, now gone gray with sweat and dust. "Yeah," he answered. "Pretty much."

James rushed him then, taking Michael by the waist and pushing him back against the bed to attack him with hot, fierce kisses. Something about that cocky streak ate at James, something about the way he grinned and accepted him for what he was. "Good thing—" James huffed between kisses, yanking open the remaining buttons to find heated flesh underneath. "—you're a stuffy, self-absorbed Corporate kiss ass." He smiled against Michael's lips, giving a hard tug at his trousers when he felt him smile back.

"Sex," Michael said, dragging his blunted fingernails up James's back, catching faded old scars and sweaty skin. "I haven't been with anyone in a while."

Letting out a soft moan of encouragement, James pressed a line of kisses to Michael's ear before whispering, "Me neither. I won't tell if you don't."

Michael laughed then and murmured something sounding like 'deal' before introducing his lips to James's throat. They were both worn thin with the whole situation, and it showed, but helped to not think about being lost and arguing over it. It was nice for James to feel lips caressing down his neck to his shoulder as he then found Michael's scarred arm. Michael paused, his body unmoving underneath James's larger form, until James began brushing featherlight kisses over the mark with deliberate care, the same care he felt when Michael's fingers traced the line where flesh met metal. Michael lifted his hips to meet above James's knee, ardent hardness pitching against James as though Michael had to tell him he was pressing all the right buttons. "Want you," Michael whispered, swallowing a deep breath as James lowered the zipper on his pants. "Please."

"So polite." James answered and then dragged his tongue up the length of Michael's fading scar before pushing up onto his knees to look down at him. "You don't even know how sexy you are, do you?"

Michael turned his face toward the worn pillow under his head, no doubt hiding a blush as he lifted his hips to slide off his clothes and fully expose thin legs leading up to a nest of blond curls at the base of his rising cock. "Shut up."

James slid down on the bed, and then onto his belly to caress Michael's thighs with stubbled cheeks as he murmured, "Never." It was truth—few things could render James Marks speechless, but Michael was getting pretty good at figuring them out. Thin fingers wound in James's unkempt hair, wrapping the strands into Michael's fist as he pushed James closer to his goal. James was more than happy to oblige Michael in the moment. They'd been working up to it on the train, those tentative kisses promising that things were just starting to get interesting. James's lips brushed up Michael's inner thigh and he inhaled deeply, taking in the heady scent and taste of sweat and lust, before finding his way to Michael's balls, gently kissing that tender skin with same reverence as any other kiss. His tongue darted and lapped, tasting him, drinking in every moment.

Michael seemed a little more to the point and grasped his cock by the base, squeezing tightly as he guided the tip against James's lips. He stroked back the skin with a quick slide of his hand, letting out a hiss of breath when James suckled the tip gently, drawing only that much between his lips. "Fuck." Michael breathed, his grip in James's hair loosening only a moment before trying to press down for more.

With a long, focused lick, James pulled back and offered him a wicked grin. "Well, if you insist..."

Michael groaned and gave another rough push. "Please?"

"I will never get tired of hearing that." James caved in to his own desire as much as Michael's, taking him in fully to feel the length swell and pulse against his tongue as Michael pushed toward his throat. Holding him there for a long moment, James swallowed and fast. Michael's hips bucked, forcing another hard swallow before fading to a slow and easy lift and fall against the unexpectedly soft bed. James let him set the pace, allowing himself to take the moment in and enjoy the soft cries sticking in Michael's throat.

Suddenly, Michael pulled James back by a fistful of shaggy brown hair—the tingle of pain along his scalp shooting straight down to his cock and making the pressure against James's zipper all the more real. "S-st-stop," Michael panted, licking dry lips. He forced himself up and grabbed James's waist with both arms, tugging at him as though he could lift James's thick body. "Pants off."

"Now that"—James remarked, already following the order—"is how you ask a guy to take his pants off."

"Get your coat. I know it's in there."

James didn't bother pretending he didn't know what Michael was talking about. "Hey now, I've got to protect my image as an intergalactic man slut somehow." James laughed, but Michael didn't even crack a smile. "Can't be too prepared, right?"

Michael didn't answer, merely caught the slim bottle James tossed to him and then flipped open the cap to apply the slick liquid to his cock. "You're slowing me down."

"I like a guy who knows what he wants," James said, sliding back on the bed. His jeans crumpled to the floor, and he knelt across Michael's lap. "But you already knew that."

For a moment, Michael was intent on staring at James's bare skin, his eyes lingering on James's chest and then following the trail of dark hair that spread across his chest and belly down to where his cock smeared a bead of wetness against Michael's navel. Then, he said, "I like you, too, James."

"Clearly—" James had more on his tongue, but it was cut off by the hard prod of the tip of Michael's cock forcing him open. "Fuck...that's..."

"Good?" He huffed, lifting his hips to slowly push into James.

James nodded, incapable of forming actual words for a few seconds, and then pushed Michael down with his weight. Thankfully, he allowed James to wrest control of the moment, and James let Michael's cock fill him, stretching him open with one long push that left him shaking as he took it all in. Michael's hand slid along James's waist to his thighs, losing all subtlety as he gripped on each side, one flesh, one unyielding metal. "You like it, don't you?" James managed, leaning in to slowly rock back against him.

Michael turned his head away again, and James knew he didn't have to answer that question. In a way, the silent admission made him enjoy the sensation of Michael bucking up against him even more. "It's okay," James said, brushing a kiss on Michael's forehead as he angled himself to dig his cock against Michael's soft, hairless belly with each stroke. "I don't mind."

"I've never met anyone like you," Michael answered and then looked back up at James with a flushed, grinning face.

James grunted, working his palm between them to tug his cock against Michael's smooth skin, letting him feel the streaks of his arousal as he sped up the pace of their steady grinding. "Don't think, Michael. Just enjoy the ride."

Both of Michael's hands slid up James's hips once more and then to his back until finally he gripped tight around James's torso. Michael's body shook only a second and then seized as he let go with a hollow groan and frantic draw of breath. His fine lashes fluttered behind his dusty spectacles, and James settled back to watch the warmth flush across his face as Michael's come filled him. "James…" he whispered, hands pantomiming as though grabbing for shoulders out of his reach when James reclined astride his lap.

"Shh…" James grinned down at Michael, squeezing hard around the shaft of his cock as he stroked hard and fast. Michael didn't make another sound until James had stroked his own fluids onto Michael's stomach, marking him like an animal.

Michael reached down, tentatively touched James's scars, and said, "I'm pretty sure you're crushing my pelvis."

Rolling off Michael onto the first comfortable bed James had felt in over a year, he laughed and buried his head Michael's his shoulder. "Ahh, 'm not that heavy…" He managed with a chuckle stifled against Michael's skin. Dragging a kiss over the tang of sweat and dust, he added, "Just need to do a little more practice."

For a moment, Michael didn't respond. He breathed deeply, and then took off his glasses and reached over James to fold them onto the side table. He said, "I think we could manage that."

The softness in Michael's voice was unexpected, a far cry from the bitter frustration he'd been mostly hearing out of him. James kissed him again, his arms drawing Michael to lay across his broad chest. The stillness between them was comfortable, but James had a question that tickled at his curiosity. "Why haven't you been fucking?" he asked without shame. "I mean, cute guy like you probably had a lot of options, even locked up in the dome like that."

Michael chuffed and didn't say anything for several moments. He answered with the same earnest tone. "Stories spread fast. I guess a lot of people knew what I did...what I didn't do. It wasn't really a big deal; jerking off means you don't have to talk about things."

James nodded and brushed a kiss in the sweat-matted hair at Michael's temple. "Fair enough."

"What about you? Mister 'I have a reputation.' Are you really going to tell me people aren't throwing themselves at you?"

James's lips quirked into a lopsided smile. "Lost a few good guys over the last few years. Bounty hunters got 'em, mostly, or settling down. Got sick of rolling a stranger I'd never see again in some shithole small mining town. After a while, guess it made more sense to go it alone; at least I know I can trust the person I'm with."

"Is that why you didn't have anyone with you at the facility?" Michael shifted against him, eventually finding a place to rest his head on James's shoulder. "Nobody you can trust?"

James's fingers idly stroked through Michael's hair, pulling out a few dirty tangles with a gentle touch. "Anyone ever told you you think too much?"

Michael chuckled and kissed James's shoulder. "Hint taken."

Five: Calling Out

THEY DOZED THROUGH the first warm hours of twilight, content to simply enjoy the quiet company and what had happened between them, for better or worse. As the evening cool set in, James roused Michael from bed to what passed for a shower on most water-deficient planets.

"C'mon," James groaned, tugging at Michael's elbow to drag him into the tiny stall sectioned off in one corner of the small room. "You ever hear of a microbial shower?"

"Sounds like hot water and lots of soap." Michael sighed, glancing around the cubicle. "And I don't see evidence of either."

Compelled, knowing it would do little to ease Michael's transition into new territory, James kissed the top of his head. "Yeah...see, a lot of planets out here have to scrape for water, and using it to wash is seen as a luxury for those with money to waste." James reached out and slammed his fist against the single innocuous red button before either of them could back out. "So they found a way to get rid of bacteria and such without using any water."

The cubicle door slid closed with a hollow sound, leaving little room for them to move as the sticky green sludge began to pour in from a pipe near the base. "This is actually pretty nice," James said. "Usually it's six or seven of us all crammed in together when this part happens. This is almost romantic."

"I'm, uh...ah...a little nervous about the whole goo aspect?" Michael looked up at him, and James caressed his cheek and ran a thumb across his lips before offering a peck of a kiss.

"Don't swallow any, and you'll be fine."

Michael's eyes widened as the pipe began to pump the microbes in faster, the goo already starting to track up their legs. "Swallow?"

"Yeah, in about a minute we'll be in over our heads for ten seconds before the heat cleanse."

"I really don't like the sound of that." Michael frowned, looking up to apparently avoid looking down at the goo climbing his thighs.

Feeling the slickness sliding up inside him, cleaning out the evidence of their earlier encounter, James couldn't stifle a small laugh. "Oh! Tickles a little bit..."

"My skin is *literally* crawling right now."

"Close your eyes and take a deep breath... You're about neck high. When you feel the heat, you'll know it's safe to breathe again." James took his own deep breath, keeping both eyes on Michael until he felt the tingle crawling up his jaw.

The heat hit with a full-body sting that left them both tinged pink and tender. "What in the fresh hell..." Michael shouted, only to be cut off as James kissed him again.

"You did good," James said, brushing both hands across Michael's warm cheeks, smiling reflexively when he opened his eyes. "My first time I screamed like a baby and almost choked to death. I mean, I was six at the time...but, you know..."

Michael nodded. "Yeah, all right. I guess that was a thing that we did."

The cubicle door slid open, and James let him escape first to get another look at Michael's thin body before he found his pants again. "I need to head out for a little while. You should probably stay here."

"Is that your way of saying you're gonna skip out and leave me here, now that we've had a little fun, and I probably couldn't turn you in before your ship gets here?" Michael looked up at James, after locating his glasses and slipping them on, brows furrowed in a look that spoke of genuine worry.

"No." James really hadn't even thought of that; his style wasn't fuck and run, even when things weren't exactly looking great. "It's my way of saying there are a lot of people here who would be very willing to fill you full of holes of the much less fun type if they find out you're a Peach employee."

"So, they don't find out?" Michael shrugged on his shirt. "I don't exactly feel safe being here alone either."

James sighed and sat after slipping into his somewhat stiff jeans. "Look, I need to call my ship so they can come and rescue us. You...okay, you see how I look? Long hair, kinda permanently filthy, *weathered* if you will?"

"Yeah..."

"Well, you look like the opposite of that. And folks out here see that as either being a threat, or someone they can rob." Michael frowned at him. "Don't get me wrong! I think you are absolutely adorable. And I do mean that. But, if I was looking for a schmuck I wouldn't feel too bad about stabbing in the face and robbing blind, I'd probably find someone like you."

Michael's frown deepened. "So I'm too attractive to go out?"

"Yeah, pretty much. No offense intended."

"And now I hate you again." Michael folded his arms over his chest and turned his back to James as he put on his own clothes.

"You don't have to hate me; it's just the truth. I'm trying to protect you here. These people don't know you. All they know is that corporations like Peach fuck them over at every turn and make a living off their backs while doing it. They see the corporations as nothing but overpowered bullies who want to be gods. Do you get that?"

"I *get* that you think I can't protect myself, and you don't trust me."

"I trust you fine; it's those other assholes that're unpredictable." Michael didn't reply, and James didn't press the issue any harder as he tugged on his boots. "I won't be long. Just gonna call in my coordinates and maybe see if I can find us something more appetizing than another protein bar. Okay?"

"Fine," Michael muttered in response, running a hand through his hair.

***

Making the call was simple enough with access to a reliable data uplink. Most crews, James's included, tried to use person to person when they could, since it was more secure. Unfortunately, it required you to be within a thousand kilometers of the person you were trying to reach. Out of that range, the only way was with a satellite uplink, which of course meant it would be broadcast over Corporate-owned networks and had to be coded in a way that didn't raise any red flags.

James attached his jack and slid into the booth, drawing the curtain closed for what little privacy was afforded in the busy saloon. As he guided the port into position, he briefly thought of Michael and the situation James had put them both in. As far as Peach was concerned, they probably figured James was a kidnapper, who took off with their assistant head of R&D, and an attempted thief on top of that. It didn't really matter much. In the long run, it was only a matter of time before he ended up with a price attached to his identity like every other outlander in the galaxy who didn't settle into mining or set up shop somewhere steady. What James really cared about was what Michael thought; that twinge of guilt about leaving him alone in the room welled up, and he forced it back to dial directly to the ship's computer.

Calling up his HUD, James could picture the crew watching the hack come through, maybe assuming the worst—that he'd been caught and probably killed on sight. James tapped their security code into the HUD with his mind, focusing on the outgoing message. Only the coordinates and situation.

2x cargo for p/u. Rush job.

It was simple enough and let them know all they needed to know: two needing collecting in a hurry. James waited, hoping for some kind of reply. After a few minutes passed, the yellow warning light flashed beyond his peripheral vision, letting him know he'd nearly overstayed his welcome in the booth. Then, as he unplugged, a short message confirmed.

En route. ETA 12 hours.

James hadn't even drawn back the curtain, admittedly a little proud of himself and his crew for having their shit together when they needed it to work, when he heard a familiar voice cry out. "I don't even have anything worth stealing!"

"Fuck..." James muttered under his breath as he stepped out, scanning over the tight crowd through a circle of burly men to see Michael doubled over on his knees with his face against the floor.

"Stop yer screaming, little pig." A particularly nasty looking merc in a cliché black hat spat in the dust near Michael's head. "Who you working for? Trinicore? Alpha Corps? Peach?"

James shouted out, "He works for me, asshole. And I'd appreciate you backing the hell off my property."

Several of the men chuckled, glancing at James before glowering down at Michael. "Well lookie here...if it isn't another loser trying to get in on our take. Fuck off." The apparent leader kicked Michael in the side, rolling him onto his back. "Check his pockets, Curly. Bet he's got ID on him, in case he gets caught spying."

"I wasn't spying!" Michael protested. "I...I was looking for my...my master!" He wriggled and rolled away from the meaty hands groping toward him.

Pushing through the gathered group into the circle, James grabbed Michael by the collar, hauling him to his feet. "I paid for him fair and square..." He stared down the leader, swallowing back his own fear of being turned into a pile of skin and metal. With a sweep of one steady hand, James brushed back his duster to show off the ElectroPistol on his hip. "Don't make me break the law on my first night in town."

"First and last," the leader answered, going for his gun.

With all the self-preservation he could muster, James dropped Michael and had his ElectroPistol on the beefy asshole's head before he could raise his old tech junker. "Last chance, jackass. You and your boys can walk out of here, or I can drop you and start a whole load of shit for all of us."

The leader swallowed, considering his options, apparently. It was a hell of a gambit but one that had to pay off, or things were going to get even worse for both of them.

"Hey now! You get the hell out of here!" the proprietor shouted, coming out from behind the bar with an ancient-looking shotgun. "I will end this."

Taking a deep breath, the stranger let out a soft, dry laugh as he holstered his weapon. "Just doin' business, Mister Milkea. Rumor is there's a Peach boy on the run...little guy here fit the description."

"You don't go hasslin' my customers, or their servants. Now git with you lot, or I'm gonna start blasting."

"He's not the only one," James added, curling his lower lip. He slid back the lever, hearing the whine as his weapon powered up. "I've turned men to dust for less."

"Yeah, yeah, fine. Don't gotta go all sheriff on me, scav." The stranger spat on the floor and turned away from James. "Watch your back, piggy."

They both held their breath until the tavern door slammed shut. The owner broke the tension. "You two better get on, too; you're paid for now, but I don't want to see you again come morning."

Michael led the way, yanking at the sleeve of James's jacket until they were safely in the room before letting out a growled, angry cry. "You should have blown his fucking head off."

"Well, yeah, I could have done that..." James sighed, throwing himself onto the bed. "And completely blown away all hope of making it off this rock alive."

Michael didn't answer, only stood there and stared for a long moment. Then he said, "Whatever. Go ahead, let me have it. I followed you. I got caught like you said I would."

James looked up at him, catching his eyes behind the thin spectacles, and then rolled onto his back and closed his eyes against the pounding of his pulse. Truth was, he hadn't shot anyone in a good long while, and didn't particularly look to change that any time soon. "I'm just glad everything went fine."

James heard Michael's footsteps on the wooden floor, hesitant and slow. Then Michael's light weight sank to the side of the bed. The din downstairs started anew, building up as a terrible band began to play, but their room was silent until James was almost asleep. In a soft voice, Michael said, "What even are you? Those guys wouldn't have hesitated to drop either of us."

"Just a guy," James answered with a heavy sigh. "Look, I know you met me in kinda weird circumstances, but most of us out here are trying to survive. I'm not sayin' I'm a good guy, but I ain't like *them* either."

Michael huffed, and then, surprisingly, lay beside him. "So, your ship is coming?"

"Yeah. They got the message."

James waited for him to ask what comes next, but he didn't. Instead, they dozed again in the warm embrace of postpanic and the evening routine until a small breakfast was brought in the late morning. After that, it was time to get walking.

Six: *SIO*

THEY LEFT TOWN in the late morning with a belly full of meat and bread that would have made James's crew jealous if they ever found out. As it was, they had a hell of a hike to the closest empty stretch of packed dirt where the ship could safely land.

"They'll be in range soon," James told Michael as they walked. "They'll pick up my signal once they enter orbit."

"Short range?" Michael looked up to him, brows knit together. "I haven't seen short-range tech in a decade."

"Sure you have," James answered with a grin. "Surprised you didn't notice the modifications in my, uh...enhancements."

Michael laughed, and the sound cut through James like a refreshing breeze across the sand. "Yeah, well, when I programmed my diagnostic routine, I didn't think I'd be working with ancient technology."

"Hey now, careful what you're calling *ancient*. That tech is gonna get us out of here without having to use Corporate satellite systems again."

"Guess you con men think of everything." Michael's sideways glance held a teasing smirk, and James couldn't help but put an arm around his shoulder as they briefly picked up their pace.

Slowing his steps again some time later, James answered, "It's really barely enough to work circles around the delightful hurdles that the corporations put up for folks trying to make a living."

"Yeah, a living. A living of cheating, lying, stealing…"

"I would *never* cheat. No fun in that."

Michael stopped for a second, looking up at James with his confused and exasperated smirk. "Yeah, well—"

"Not that the rest of my crew feels the same way, mind you. Just don't agree to play cards with them. Or nails. Or anything at all, really."

"They sound great," Michael replied dryly.

James didn't really have a response to that. He knew his crew wasn't necessarily the easiest to get along with, but they were loyal, and in an age where you could hardly tell the difference between friend and enemy, it made for welcome company.

Keeping watch on the horizon, they found a large rock to give a generous enough amount of shade as they waited for the ship. "Let me do the talking, okay? There's a couple of my people who tend to shoot first and ask questions later when Peach is involved."

"What did the Corporations ever do to them?" Michael looked up, swabbing his forehead with his sleeve.

James frowned, leaning into the relative coolness of the rock with a hollow sigh. "Oh, you know…espionage, murder, a couple tours of the worst prison colony in Corporate Space. Siblings. They lost their family a few decades back because they refused untested upgrades. You're not even close to the only person they've fucked over."

Michael's mouth opened as though he had something to say, but no words came out. Instead, he sipped at the remnants of their water and closed his eyes.

"I know *you* didn't pull the trigger; you're…well, you're nobody. Nothing personal."

Michael sighed. "Fair enough."

James didn't really know what he'd hoped to get out of Michael, maybe a glimmer of a smile or some indication that he wasn't totally miserable, despite the circumstance. Staring up at the sky, he saw the blip drag up his HUD well before they saw the burn trail entering the atmosphere.

Calling up the short range, James opened the communication channel. "I see my darling SIO!" he exclaimed, knowing Corin would pick it up well before Edge or Razor. "You picking up coordinates? I'm dyin' out here."

"You've got a tail, boss." Corin's soft purr in James's ear drew an instant smile to his face. "Must be off your game."

"Not a tail, Princess. It's complicated," he replied, offering a hesitant smile when Michael looked at him with a confused eyebrow raised.

"No shit, it's complicated. We're running on reserves to get out to Hell's Asshole here. I take it things are the kind of fucked-up where we're not getting paid?"

James sighed, shaking his head for Michael's benefit. "I'll work it out with Lyra, but we could really use a drink and some grub."

"When I said we're runnin' on reserves, I didn't mean only gas. We can't take on another mouth to feed without getting paid."

"C'mon, Corin. You're starting to sound like Lyra."

She sighed, and for a second, James was sure she was going to close the channel. "Fuck you, James."

"Okay, I earned that. We'll figure it out, okay? Have I ever let you down?"

"Want me to wait to answer that until your little friend can hear?"

Cowed, James closed his eyes again and leaned heavily into the rock. "Just pick us up, please? We'll hash it out once I'm not baking out here."

EDGE AND RAZOR flanked the door as James walked up the gangway, Michael trailing several strides behind. They didn't look amused, understandably so.

"I can explain everything." James answered the unasked questions written on his crew's well-worn faces. "Give me a minute to get a drink."

It was Edge who moved first, waiting until James had passed them to cock his old pistol and point it down the ramp at Michael's head. "He ain't coming aboard."

James reached out and placed a hand over the barrel, looking up at his crewman. They'd known each other a long time, and James knew he had his reasons for not trusting anyone who looked like they came fresh out of Corporate Space. "Come on, Edge. Trust me."

The familiar whirr of an ElectroPistol powering up came from behind, and James felt Razor's weapon digging into his back. "Trust you? Do you have any idea how fucked we are right now?"

"No more fucked than we've been before," James answered quickly, making no move to stop her. For all of Edge's strength, it was his sister who was cold as ice. James didn't doubt, for a second, he'd already be dead if she didn't have a scrap of trust left. "I told Corin already, I'll talk to Lyra. I'll fix this. Why do you think I took a hostage?"

James could feel Michael's eyes boring into him, well aware of the shock of hearing he'd been betrayed. There wasn't much choice in the matter; if they knew James was saving Michael's ass as much as his own, they wouldn't have hesitated to shoot him. "You fucking prick." Michael swore loudly, a brief glance catching the view of his hands lifting up and clasping behind his head. "You wouldn't kill an unarmed man. Would you?"

James swallowed the lump in his throat, his pulse racing until Razor's weapon slowly dropped away from his back. "She would."

Razor scoffed, and James kept his eyes on Edge, listening to Razor's short strides down the metal ramp as she gathered Michael. "Give me a good reason not to drop you where you stand."

"We need him," James answered for him, a little surprised at the curious look in Edge's eyes. "He's the assistant head of R&D for Peach. What he knows is worth more than the Rose to Lyra, assuming he can't figure us a way out of this, and he's no good to us dead." It was all truth, for the little it mattered. As much as the crew needed the money, he wasn't about to turn over anyone to their benefactor—cash in hand or not.

There was a heavy thud and Michael cried out only once, before Razor grumbled, "Put him in the tank. You have a lot of explaining to do, *Captain*."

"In the morning," James sighed, finally turning back to face the cargo hold of his ship, satisfied nobody was in immediate danger of getting shot. "It's been a rough couple days."

"It's not gonna get any easier, James." It was Corin's sweet voice that met him head-on. James looked up to see her standing in the open cockpit doorway—watching what had happened, no doubt. "She's meeting us here tonight."

"Tonight?" James asked, already shaking his head. "You couldn't hold her off a while longer? She's your mother. Use her...I don't know, her motherly instinct."

"My mother," Corin seethed, "has all the motherly instinct of a cockroach. You know her better than that. The second you were running late she ran our coordinates and locked on. Her speeder may have been farther out than we were, but unlike some boats, she ain't trying like hell to conserve power."

James covered his face with one hand, doing little to hide or relieve the dissatisfying truth of the matter. "All right…I can do this. We can handle this."

"Damn right we can," Edge answered, with a bellowing grunt, as he dumped Michael's unconscious body in the makeshift holding cell and powered up the electric bars. "If this guy's as valuable as you say, maybe she'll pay even more than the contract."

"Right." James swallowed a sigh, unable to take his eyes off the dark split on Michael's scalp blossoming blood into his short blond hair. "What about you? I guess none of you want to be here when Lady Lyra shows her face."

"Shit no. She scares me," Edge answered, squaring his wide shoulders. "Woman's a scorpion."

"She's a broker." Razor slugged her big brother in the side before taking his elbow. "We're all potential gold to her. Nothing more."

"We'll head into town. You can chat with dear old Mom." Corin sighed loudly, frowning back at them. "You fix this, James, or we're done. I'm walking, and without a good pilot, you may as well sell this piece of shit."

Seven: The Plan

JAMES GATHERED WHAT little medical supplies were left on board and waited until his crew's shadows had dropped away toward Aurora before cutting the power to the cell, lowering the force field. Sitting beside Michael's unconscious form was a hell of a switch up, and James would almost prefer their situations be reversed. Razor had hit Michael hard at the temple, the mark on his hairline not much more than a small split that soaked through two pads of gauze before slowing enough to bandage him. James couldn't explain why, but he held Michael in his lap, stroking the streaks of drying blood out of his hair until he began to come to and struggled to focus his eyes.

"So…" Michael said dryly, squinting until James slid his, thankfully, unscathed glasses onto his face. "Was it your plan all along?"

James looked down at Michael, and then at the mess of bloodied gauze beside him. "No. And it's not my plan now."

"Right, so you lied to your whole crew to protect someone you tried to rip off three days ago? Somehow, I'm skeptical." Michael frowned and then leaned his head back and closed his eyes with a weary sigh.

It was complicated. Doing the right thing sometimes meant a few lies to people you cared about. In the end, the crew always understood James did what he had to do. "It doesn't matter." James sighed, shaking his head. "Our benefactor is going to be here in a few hours, and I don't have the Rose...or anything else for that matter. My ship is dead in the water, and my crew is ready to walk. Why would I bother lying to you if I was going to turn you over anyway?"

For a minute, Michael looked like he was going to answer James's question. Then, he shook his head and sighed. "So what's the plan?"

"I don't know," James answered honestly. "I guess I'll probably have to kill her." The thought made him shudder. Sure, Lyra and James had their differences over the years, but she was just another person trying to make their way in an unforgiving world. A very powerful person with a lot of money and a lot of connections, but a person, no less.

"Guess that's always on the table," Michael replied sourly.

"Not really, no. I haven't actually killed anyone in...well..." James's hand lifted up subconsciously, closing over the chip hidden in his inner coat pocket. "I killed the bounty hunter who used the kill code."

Michael grew quiet and then sat up slowly, rocking a little as he fought the dizziness. He took shallow breaths and closed his eyes, and after a long moment, James asked, "Gonna be okay?"

Michael shook his head negative. In a soft, wavering voice he said, "You should hand me over. I know everything your benefactor wants to know."

James couldn't bring himself to go that far down the rabbit hole of outlander politics, not that he really expected Michael to understand the situation. "I'll think of something and get you back where you belong."

Michael groaned and then looked right at James, eyes wide and red-rimmed behind his glasses. "At least if you turn me over to her, I'll live. I think you know what Peach does to rogue employees."

"You ain't rogue. You were kidnapped; you said it yourself."

He swallowed hard. "Yeah, maybe with anyone else they may take that at face value. But I'm not exactly...I mean...I'm..."

It dawned on James as Michael stumbled over his words. "You're a prisoner."

Lowering his eyes, Michael nodded slowly. "I tried, James. I should be—"

James's HUD pulled up Michael's ident file, double-checking himself before he opened his mouth. At the top, flashing red, were the words in all caps: KILL ON SIGHT. "Dead."

"Yeah. They can't trust I didn't spill all their secrets. I may as well do some good with what I know. I can tell this Lyra person everything Peach knows about the Rose, or any of the other projects I was working on, really. I've been busy for the last few years."

"She doesn't deserve your brain." James leaned in and kissed Michael again, drinking in the soft surprise of his mouth before he pulled away.

"I don't have anywhere else to go. I mean, it's not like I ever planned to do anything but what I was doing for the rest of my life." Michael shrugged, a pink flush creeping up under his collar where his pale skin had started to brown.

"You could always stay with me." James let out an awkward laugh. He'd never really been as great with men as his reputation implied, especially not the sort who didn't spend a good deal of their life doing nothing but trying not to die, and it felt like a rather too flirtatious thing to even say. "Could always use a tech guy on my crew."

"Your crewman tried to kill me."

Michael's bluntness drew an unexpected smirk out of James and he answered, "Razor? No, if she had tried to kill you, you'd be dead. She knocked you out. She does that. She's knocked me out at least five times."

"At least?"

"After the first few times, your memory gets to be not...so...uh...good."

Michael laughed, and the knot in James's gut began to slowly unravel. James added, "I'll think of something. I always do."

Reaching out to steady himself on James's shoulder, Michael pushed to his feet and attempted a shaky step. "Careful," James cautioned. "Concussions are nasty."

"Do you have a lab or anything like one? Somewhere with wires or metal work?"

Raising an eyebrow, James followed after him, picking up the mess he'd left behind on the way. "Not really. I mean, Corin has a workbench for when something on ship breaks."

"That'll do." Michael looked around the cargo hold, following James's lead as he pointed toward Corin's corner. Michael found the bench with ease and started pulling out various bits and bobs that James would be hard-pressed to identify as anything other than "that engine thing or whatever."

"Right. So I'll bite. What exactly are you doing?" James approached slowly from behind, watching Michael's soft hands pry open a round thing with wires and circuits inside.

"Only *maybe* a dozen employees and test subjects have actually seen the Rose, and I'm one of the few who know what it does who aren't currently wearing prisoner ID tags." Michael spoke in a quiet, clipped tone, disconnecting the wires before he dug into a box of miscellaneous wires, screws, and metal pieces that Corin used for smaller repairs. "All we have to do is make something that looks fancy enough to be a Corporate secret and spin enough technobabble that your boss is sufficiently impressed."

"And you can do this in two hours?" James was suitably impressed; he wouldn't normally even think of trying to pull a quick one on Lyra.

Michael looked back at him for a second and flashed a small wary smile before going back to his work. "Promise me you'll make sure your crew doesn't kill me?"

"Are you kidding? You pull my ass out of the fire, I'll marry you."

"Not dying will do." Michael shook his head. "Hand me my kit."

James fetched the small tool set that had fallen to the wayside after Razor smacked Michael on the head. He was content to watch Michael work, clearly out of his depth. In Michael's mind the plan seemed to make sense, and given that James had no other plan to fall back on, it was good enough to do.

Michael's voice was barely a whisper as he muttered to himself. He pushed his glasses up on the bridge of his nose as he worked, eyes watching the circuitry as it all clicked into place. "Here, touch this," he said well over an hour later, shoving the roughly oval-shaped device James's direction.

"Promise it won't send me to another planet?" James was mostly joking...but only mostly.

"Sure."

"That's not very comforting."

Michael sighed. "Neither is knowing someone who would probably have no problem destroying both of us could show up any time. Worst-case scenario, it'll fry your circuits, not really kill you."

"Good. Nice." James stalled only a moment before taking a deep breath and grasping the orb with his palm. Nothing happened.

"Fuck." Michael frowned, his fingers absently stroking the fine creases along the corners of his mouth. "Okay, don't let go yet."

"Oh...kay..." James's eyes widened, and Michael turned his wrist, the weight of the device settling in his palm as Michael dug into it again, pressing the button on a tiny soldering tool to fuse a green wire into a circuit. That, it seemed, produced the desired effect—which from James's end of the equation was first a bright-purple flash of light, and then, picking himself up off the floor.

"What did you press?" Michael asked quickly, grasping James by the wrist to hold the device still in his tightly clenched fingers. "Tell me you pressed the button."

"There's a button?" James whined, unable to easily move his clenched jaw.

"Sort of, yeah. It produced a really interesting electrical current. I wasn't expecting that." Michael took off his glasses, lowered them to the table, and then rubbed the bridge of his nose. "Where did this circuit board come from?"

"I..." James trailed off as he reached up and rubbed hard across his jaw stubble until he felt the muscles start to unclench. "You think I know that? I haven't even looked at half this junk in years."

"Junk?" Michael's eyes shot up, locking on James's as his frown deepened. "This junk is saving our lives. Just so you know."

It was all James could do not to reach out to him and make it clear that while nobody else might see it, he was well aware it wasn't the junk saving any of them; it was Michael and his precious brain. Michael's knowledge and his situation, for however much James had fucked it up personally, were going to make everything better.

Suddenly, Michael's eyes narrowed, and then he glanced toward the open cargo door as the familiar hum of a shuttle drew near. "I hope it's enough," he whispered. "You should let me do the talking this time."

Eight: Lyra

THERE WASN'T TIME to discuss the actual plan, let alone how they were going to pull it off. Michael put on his glasses, took the orb from James, and then slid his hand against James's belly and into his duster to grab the ElectroPistol. "Don't shoot me," he said before pressing it into James's hand. "I trust you."

It was that trust that allowed James to swallow back the nerves rising in his throat. He'd spun a lot of shit in his day, a whole lot more than any strictly sane person should, mind you, but he'd never had the sac on his own to shove a line down the throat of the woman who lately had single-handedly funded the ship's little merry band of outlanders. They were in a small shuttle, and for a moment, James hoped she might be alone, but he wasn't surprised to see a pair of bodyguards marching up the gangway before her.

"Secure the ship!" Lyra's voice barked. "My daughter's fond of little surprises."

James drew in a deep breath and squeezed his fingers tighter around the grip of his ElectroPistol, feeling it hum to life under his palm, once more. It was the second time in twenty-four hours he'd aimed the gun at a person he had no actual intention of killing—he had a good run going. "Lyra, darling! Gentlemen, nice to see you again."

"Shut up, James," the gray-skinned leader of her personal guard growled at him. "Where's the crew?"

"Shore leave. You think I'm going to let them *hang out* when I have a top-secret device in my possession?" James replied on autopilot, watching as the lady herself began to ascend the ramp.

Lyra's dingy blonde hair was curled into a severe bun, with several pins and other implements jutting out at various points, and it offset the dark-gray gown that clung to her generous curves. Her voice held a menacing timbre. "Don't try to be funny, James. I know they probably ditched your sorry ass as soon as you tried to come up with yet *another* reason you fucked up *another* simple job."

"Hey, I didn't fuck this one up! There were a few setbacks—" James protested, only to be surprised when Michael jumped in.

"I slowed him down." Michael looked straight at her, holding the orb against his chest. "The Rose doesn't go anywhere without me."

"And as you may have noticed," James cut back in, "I was right in the middle of explaining that his work on the project was done."

"Wait..." Lyra held up a hand, her eyes once more taking in the empty cargo hold as her men stood one to the left of the main entrance and the other in front of the cockpit door. "You work for Peach Corp?" She lowered the dark sunglasses perched already low on her tiny nose.

"Yes, ma'am," Michael replied, not taking his eyes off of her.

The head guard droned, "Name, Michael Bennet. Assistant Head of Research and Development with Peach Corp. Currently...oh, you gotta see this." There was a small flash, and the guard extended his hand, opening his palm to call up a holographic tablet that he pushed in front of his employer, displaying the HUD he'd been reading.

James didn't need to ask what they were looking at. Michael was definitely a wanted man. "Oooh. Now that is interesting," Lyra cooed. "James, I know you're not exactly shy about traveling with folks who've had some trouble in Corporate Space, but this boy..." She trailed off with a laugh, looking Michael over with a curious eye. "Hoo! You pissed off someone high up."

"This is the reason they want me." Michael held out the orb, barely cupping the bottom in his palm. "Funny how, when you disappear with top-secret technology, people tend to assume the worst."

Her attention dropped from him to the device, scrutinizing it. "This is the Rose?"

"No, it's an electromagnetic field generator that possesses the unique capacity to instantly teleport the bearer to one of an infinite number of outer-ring planets, such as the *quaint little shithole* we're currently on, but no discernable way to send them back or even figure out where they went." Michael took a deep breath. "Some idiot thought a cute name like *the Rose* made sense."

"Interesting." Lyra's eyes narrowed further, and she stepped forward until she was within grasping distance. "Michael, is it?"

"Yes," he answered firmly, without fear, not even batting an eye when Lyra brushed aside James's weapon.

"And *you* are in charge of studying this device?"

Michael shook his head and then shrugged one shoulder. "I oversaw the development of it. Testing volatile technology isn't high on my list of priorities."

"Strange words for a man on the run." Lyra laughed again, her guards joining in the moment with her. "What makes it so dangerous, little man?" Her thick hand reached out, grasping the top of the device as she took it away from him without hesitation. "It seems a little unimpressive. I mean, the layers of security I had to give James here access to, the people I had to call favors on to get to this simple little trinket for my investors..." She tossed it gingerly in her palm, letting it settle fully into her hand. "Hardly seems worth fifty thousand credits."

"Hey!" James shouted, stepping back in anticipation of the electric current that strangely didn't come. "You made a deal, Lyra. Whether you think it's worth it or not, my fee was agreed upon."

"Your fee?" She laughed again, shaking her head. "Oh James, don't you ever change... So devoted to your never-ending quest for pocket change."

"Mind the button," Michael cut in, gesturing toward the small button dangerously close to her thumb. "I'd hate for someone to accidentally activate the device."

"Oh!" she replied, clearly startled, before running her manicured nail delicately over the button. "Such a dainty thing. I'd think you would make it more difficult to activate when designing it."

Michael looked at James, and his eyes narrowed. "You'd think that. It would certainly make it less likely someone looking to steal it would end up on the other side of the galaxy, but that wasn't what the company wanted."

"Yeah, well...that's Peach for ya." James rolled his eyes, turning his attention back to Lyra. "Now, since you enjoy talking about money so much, I'll take mine now, thanks."

"Oh, shut your ass, James." Lyra groaned. "I'm about to make you a much less poor man." She stared at James, taking a step closer. "By which I mean, I've got another offer for you."

"I don't want another offer," James answered, fingers twitching on the grip of his ElectroPistol. Her glare was enough to make the hairs on the back of his neck stand up; there was never anything good to come from a counteroffer from Lyra.

"Half a million," she said sharply, glaring up at him.

James blinked, unsure of what she was telling him. "Wait. What?"

"I'd hate for this shining example of intelligence to be snuffed out when Peach Corp catches up to your ragtag little gang." She reached out, grasping Michael by his shirt collar. "I'll take the problem off your hands, and when the Corporate Police catch up to you, you'll be off free and clear."

Michael looked back at James, and his knees started to buckle. For a second there, James was pretty sure Michael thought he might actually take the offer. In all truth, James may have even considered it if he knew she wouldn't put a bullet in Michael's head the second she turned over the device to her buyer and found out he was full of shit. Hell, he'd made worse deals, but he couldn't bring himself to make that one.

"No," James said, reaching out to take the other side of Michael's collar, leaving him quivering between them. "I got plans for this one—ship needs a good brain on it. I can deal with the police. I done it before, I'll do it again, and you know it. Don't act like you're doing me a favor."

"Oh no, honey…" Lyra simply laughed it off, letting go of Michael and then looking down at her hand as though it were tainted somehow. "I don't do favors. Let's say he's worth far more to me than you'll see before you end up dead on some damn moon or something."

James knew what was coming; he didn't need enhancements to feel her goons moving in closer and to know she wasn't going to take no for an answer. "Think we'll have to agree to disagree there." Lying had always been James's strong suit; fighting was a last resort, and when he was outgunned and outclassed on both, there was nothing left but the truth. "I kinda like him. I think I'll keep him around a good long while." James's grip on Michael's collar loosened, and he wrapped an arm around Michael's shoulders, drawing him against his chest. Hell, at least if they killed James, they'd have to go through Michael first.

Michael's arms answered for him, wrapping tightly around James's waist as he let out a scared whine.

"Well," Lyra scoffed, holding up a hand to stop her bodyguards advancing. "Ain't that precious." She shook her head and laughed dryly. "You know who you're shacking up with there, Peach? He told you yet about his sob story—how he ain't a killer? He tell you what he did to the man who killed his last *friend*?"

"Drop it, Lyra. It's done. Just give me the money, and go back to your little syndicate." The lump rose up in James's throat, shaking his voice audibly. There were some things nobody needed to dredge up, least of all her.

"I think he should know." Lyra smiled broader, the lips of a jackal, as she let out another soft chuckle. "The way he clings to you, it's like you're some big man of honor. You ain't shit, James. You never have been, never will be. That bounty hunter was doing his *job*, and you tore him apart for breaking up your little love affair."

"Shut up!" James shouted, shaking and enraged at the truth even *he* didn't like to think about. In the heat of the moment, a man tended to do things he later regrets, right? "It's done, Lyra. You got something to say, you say it to Corin. I'm through being your errand boy."

Her laughter petered off to a dry chuckle, and she spat on the ship's floor. "Yeah, yeah...till you're outta money again and come running back to *mommy* for scraps." She nodded to the larger guard, and the sound of a sack of gold coin being tossed against the floor rattled in the otherwise silent bay. "You keep your boy, James. Don't come crying to me when reality catches up to you both. You ain't protected anymore, no higher horse keeping you under the radar."

James hoped she wouldn't put her daughter in enough danger to tip off the authorities, but with Lyra, anything was possible. He held his breath as she turned and walked to the end of the gangway before her guards followed carefully behind her. As soon as her shuttle buzzed to life, James let out a haggard gasp.

"She could have killed you," Michael said, breathless and shaking against James's chest. "You had two guns pointed at your head."

"Only two?" James laughed without humor. "She's losing her touch."

They didn't hear the heavy footsteps once more on the ramp, and James didn't see the bodyguard until it was too late. "Boss forgot to tell you," the gray-skinned monstrosity grunted, before a loud bang echoing through the empty metal hold. "Next time, you're both dead men."

Heat flashed across James's stomach, pain burrowing through his right side as Michael crumpled against him. Michael didn't scream, didn't even cry, only collapsed at James's feet. His head rested against James's leg as a single gasp escaped his throat.

Nine: Blood Loss

IT TOOK ALL the strength James had to drag Michael into what passed for a medical office on the ship. Getting him up on the table wasn't going to happen. James couldn't remember much in the moment, outside of feeling blood smeared and sticking down his side through jolts of piercing pain, as he tried to clean the wound through Michael's body. The ship's collection of medical supplies was a joke, but he could manage alcohol and a clean shirt pressed hard against the wound. James passed out on top, pretty damn sure they were both goners.

At least it wasn't the worst way to go.

When he came back around, James was elevated and couldn't feel Michael's smaller body under him. "Fuck!" he swore out loud, trying to force his eyes open.

"Nu-uh." Corin's voice came out sharply, somewhere close to his left side. A strong hand—Edge, James would later found out—held him down. "Gotta get the bullet out, Captain, and your boy there took the last of the knockout juice."

"Here." Razor's voice was on James's right, and something firm but yielding was pushed into his mouth. "Bite down. This is gonna hurt like a bitch."

James didn't have much choice in the matter, as pain coursed through his body, and his teeth clenched before his world all went dark again.

When James came to, he heard slow breathing in his right ear, rhythmic, but shallow. An arm was resting awkwardly above James's head, and he realized it had to be Michael's. His skin was hot against James, and James could sense a slow and steady pulse. "Michael..." James whispered, the most he could muster as broken as he felt from head to toe.

"Shh, he's still out," Corin answered, and James heard her footsteps coming closer. "Little fucker saved your life, slowed down the bullet, or it would have split your internals."

Warm relief washed over James, and he tried to tell himself it was the near-death experience talking. "Alive?"

"Yeah. You guys lost a lot of blood, but from the look of it, when we showed up, you saved his ass too—slowed the bleeding at least."

James opened his eyes to blackness, feeling the panic rise in his chest. "My TechEye's acting up."

"Your port was damaged when Edge punched you in the face," she answered. "After you woke up while I was pulling the bullet out."

"I don't..."

"He hit you really fucking hard. You've probably got a hell of a concussion too."

James sighed and closed his eyes again, trying to force himself to relax. "Where are we?"

"Headed for Corporate Space."

"Are you fucking kidding me? Who made that call?" James tried to sit bolt upright, but the pain forced him back to the flat metal surface.

"I did," Razor answered, making James aware of her presence in the room. "We've got enough heat on us without carting around Peach Corp's most wanted."

"No," James growled, knowing full well, in his current state, he had all the force of a wounded kitten. "That's not an option. Turn around; head for anywhere else. I don't fucking care."

"James—" Corin cut in. "Look, I get you feel responsible for him, but he's not our problem."

"And that bounty on his head will get us a hell of a lot farther than another job," Razor added.

"Yeah, and maybe while we're there, I'll pull the bounty on you and your brother," James spat, wishing he could see the look on her face, figuring it'd probably be pretty fucking pissed. "It's up to what...a million now?"

"You..." She stopped short of saying what everyone knew she really felt about that thought. "That's not fair."

"You wouldn't"—Corin added—"after everything they've been through with us?"

"I wouldn't, and I won't turn Michael in either. It's not up for debate. Now, go turn this bird to the nearest unaffiliated clinic before I gotta do it myself."

JAMES SLEPT, FUCK knows for how long, but he figured it had to be late when he woke again. They hadn't moved from the large metal bunk that served as the medical office's operating table and patient quarters. He was first aware of the fingers gently stroking his hair from below, and then the soft sound of someone crying. "Michael?" James asked, opening his eyes to blackness.

Michael sniffed. "Yeah, I'm here."

The fingers caressing James's head stopped, and he realized it was Michael, lying beside him. "We're alive," James said.

"Yeah," Michael answered, with a sad chuckle, and James felt the brush of short hair against his bare shoulder. "You look like shit."

"It's not every day I get punched in the face after getting shot." Through the pain, James felt Michael's fingers caress a bandage covering his temple, and then trail down James's face, finding fresh, new pools of pain. "How bad is it?"

"It'll heal," Michael answered. "Someone punched you?"

James understood the unspoken "why" in Michael's voice, but couldn't bring himself to admit the crew did the right thing and used the last of the meds on Michael and not him. "I deserved it."

A long silence passed between them, and for a moment, James thought Michael had slipped back to sleep. Then, Michael said, "Getting shot with bullets really fucking hurts."

James reached toward Michael and found the plane of his chest as he lay flat on his back. With as delicate a touch as possible, James followed the jagged taped edges of the pad covering Michael's wound down to his arm, eventually finding his fingers to wrap a weak hand around them. "I'm..." It was hard to say, but no less true. "I'm sorry for this mess."

Michael sighed, and then was silent for another long moment. Finally, he said, "Honestly? I haven't felt this *alive*, ever." He chuckled, and then let out a soft pained groan. "I think meeting you is probably the best thing that's ever happened to me."

"Big words from a man who's been knocked out cold and shot in the last twenty-four hours or so. I'm not really sure how long we were out there." There was another laughing moan, and Michael tried to move beside him. "Don't," he said, squeezing Michael's hand tighter. "You're lucky to be alive, Michael; that bullet should have killed you. Corin's a decent field stitch, but you might yet bleed out if you don't end up with an infection before we make it to a clinic."

Michael drew in a shallow breath. "Is it safe to get help?"

"Don't got much choice. If we don't, you'll probably die." It hurt James to say it, worse than the torn muscle and flesh in his side, but it was true. It was worth the risk.

"You could always...you know...let me." The words came out softly, clearly a suggestion Michael didn't want to admit.

"Sorry, Michael, not an option."

Ten: Not Dead Yet

JAMES DIDN'T LEAVE Michael's side until the crew arrived at a clinic with a reputation for working with scavs. Doctors rolled their gurneys in separate directions down a poorly lit corridor. Razor and Edge stayed with the ship, and James wasn't surprised to feel Corin's small hand on his wrist. Michael went alone.

"I'm fine!" James protested, growling and grasping out blindly as at least two doctors peeled away the gauze on his wound.

Corin ignored his protests and addressed the doctors. "They were both shot about two days ago. Bullet passed through the guy we came in with and lodged itself in James. I was able to dig out the bullet, but I'm not exactly a surgeon. He's got a TechEye and neural implant, and kind of got punched in the head a few times."

"We've got it," a low masculine voice said from somewhere above and to James's left. "Please wait outside. We'll let you know when he's ready." She protested, but left before James felt the mask come down over his face. "Try to breathe as deeply as you can," the voice said. "We'll take care of you, buddy."

James did as he was told; no sense fighting it no matter how worried he was that they were going to turn Michael over. One deep breath, then two, and then nothing at all.

When he came to, James was in the bed but could sense a much larger room around him. Voices spoke too softly to make out anything specific, but they weren't familiar. "Hel—" James's throat felt thick with sludge his tongue dry and slack as he spoke.

"Looking good, boss," Corin said from immediately beside James, once more closing her hand over his wrist. "You're all stitched up."

A cup of lukewarm water was pressed to his lips, and James drank, opening his eyes to see they weren't working yet. With a groan, he asked, "Michael?"

"He's sleeping."

As he sat up, pain rippled through James despite the meds in his system. Corin pushed against his shoulder to try to stall him, but James couldn't be stopped. "Take me to him," James said softly, adding, "Please."

Corin sighed. "Why? Why is he so important, James? He's *Peach*. We should turn him in."

"I like him," James said without thinking, without hesitating. "He needs me. I...I *need* him."

"Fuck." She sighed, guiding James up on his unsteady feet, no less. "So you're like in love with him? After a couple days?"

Dizziness almost doubled him over, but Corin slung James's arm around her broad shoulders, taking a good deal of his weight on her small frame. "I don't know." James hesitated. There was something else he needed to say, and his time alone with her was always limited. Taking his chances, James said what was on his mind. "Your mother could have killed us, probably still will."

Corin stepped forward slowly with James, setting a pace he could handle as she guided his steps. After a long moment, she asked without emotion, "Are you going to kill her?"

Honestly, James didn't know. If there was any other way to deal with her, maybe, but the options when dealing with someone who held the power she did were limited enough. "I don't want to."

They continued forward, and James slowly realized the sheer size of the recovery ward. They must have passed forty beds before she stopped him and said, "That doesn't answer my question, but I want you to know I understand if you have to. She's not the same person she was, James... She's not my mother anymore."

James nodded, but the dizziness got the better of him, sending him nearly toppling over, despite her guiding embrace. Thankfully, Corin pushed him into a chair before he could fall. "Thanks," James said, not entirely sure if it was for the help or the small comfort her blessing gave.

"Don't mention it," she answered and patted him on the shoulder. "Just...be careful."

"With Lyra or him?"

"Both."

James didn't have an answer to that; she had a valid point. He'd been through hell and back dealing with Lyra over the last few years, barely holding up his end of the bargain with the constant unspoken threat of violence or betrayal between them. Then there was Michael who recalled James's thoughts to the few times he'd allowed himself to care about someone else and watched it dissolve into pain and bloodshed. Instead of allowing himself to dwell on it, James waited until he heard her steps walking away before finding the edge of the bed in front of him, blindly sliding his hands over starched sheets until he found Michael's familiar thin hand. It was too late to be careful with him, James realized, as the warm feeling of comfort spread over him; like it or not, he was all-in as far as that matter was concerned.

JAMES DOZED OFF and on throughout the evening, holding on to Michael's limp hand. At some point a nurse brought him a little plastic cup of water and jabbed a hypo in his shoulder that made the pain ebb but didn't take it away completely. A small bell sounded somewhere far away and there was a quiet changing of the staff, but Michael did not wake.

Late in the night, small snores almost drowned out the steady hum and beep of machines around James. Michael's hand twitched, and then squeezed James's weakly. "I'm here," James murmured, half in and half out of consciousness. "Right here."

"How do I look?" Michael asked in a reedy whine James could barely hear.

James didn't have the courage to tell Michael his neural implant was broken, not in his weakened state. "Gorgeous," he answered. "I'd ravage you right here, but I think the doctors might have a problem with that."

Michael laughed and then sobbed. "Fuck it hurts..." He sighed, clinging to James's hand. "Kind of regretting that whole not-dying thing."

"Don't you dare," James shot back as forcefully as he could muster in his state. "You die and I'll have to do horrible things to your corpse."

Michael didn't answer and gradually James nodded off again. Some hours later, though he couldn't really gauge how many, James realized Michael was talking again. "Promise. James... Do you promise?"

"Hmm?" James sighed, trying like hell to remember what he'd said but drawing a blank. He answered, "Yeah, anything..."

"Don't take me back," Michael whispered, groaning low in his throat as fear overshadowed his pain. "I can't go back."

James's fingers twitched, stroking over the inside of Michael's wrist as best as he could manage in an attempt to soothe him. "I won't. We'll work it out."

A small pained sound escaped Michael's throat, and James heard the sure steps of a nurse coming between them. "I need you to lie back," a feminine voice whispered as Michael's hand let go of James's strong fingers. "Right now."

"It'll be okay, Michael," James said firmly, refusing to move from his chair despite the intrusion. "I'm not going anywhere."

Eleven: Home

ON THE SECOND day, the clinic let them go. There was nothing more they could have done that the ship's crew couldn't do with the medical supplies they'd dropped far too much gold on. Edge carried Michael up the gangway to the medical bay, and Razor took James by the elbow with them.

"You're no good like this, boss," Razor said, probably the most respectful thing James had ever heard out of her mouth.

James nodded, feeling her strong grip tighten around his elbow. "Take us home, please. Haven't been around there in a while."

"Sounds good." Edge grunted as he deposited Michael on the bunk and then the sound of heavy footsteps followed when he headed back toward the bay door.

Razor lingered but didn't speak. She guided James to the side and lifted his fingers to trace them over the edge of the bed to orient himself.

"He's gonna be okay," James said, following the cold metal to Michael's hand, up to his shoulder and then higher, to stroke his bedraggled hair. He was out again, always in and out as his body healed. "He'll fix me. Don't worry."

She sighed, and then she walked away. Alone together, James slowly sat on the edge of the bunk, as close as he could get to Michael. Moments later, Michael's soft voice asked, "What's wrong? Is your leg acting up again?"

He was caught. James could pretend and lie to him, but there was no sense in it. "I'm blind. The connection with my neural port was severed."

"Shit." Michael said. "I can't... I'm not..."

"I know," James answered, stroking his fingers through Michael's hair again, drinking in the sensation of dirty, sweaty hair under his fingers. "You're healing."

Michael didn't answer for a long moment, and again, James was sure he fell asleep. Then, Michael whispered, "You saved my life."

"Yeah, I guess so."

"Where's home?" he asked. "You told the angry one to take us home?"

Home was a place James hadn't been in some years. He deflected the question with what would pass for proper introductions, given the way Michael was brought to their happy little crew. "Her name is Razor, the angry one. I met her and her brother—the big guy, Edge—a lifetime ago. They're tough, but I've never met anyone more loyal in my life." James held his tongue at the urge to say maybe nobody before Michael, but it sounded like a bad idea even with the amount of painkillers in his system. Instead, he continued. "The short blonde, Corin— she's the whole reason this ship runs. And she hooked me up with Lyra, who I swear hasn't shot me before."

At the mention of *her* name, Michael's body went rigid beside James, and the slow trace of his fingers around the edges of the bandage stopped. "I don't want to think about that."

Leaning toward Michael as best as he could—pain be damned—James kissed what felt like a shoulder. "I'll take care of the problem."

Michael drew a ragged breath and slowly returned to the soothing touches. Sometime later, after both of them dozed off and then come around again, he said, "You never did tell me where we're going."

James, not too proud to hide, pretended to be asleep.

"HOW FAR OUT are we?" James asked, leaning heavily against the familiar copilot console. He didn't dare touch the controls, even if he did know them by heart after so many years at the helm; Corin would have run him out of the cockpit without a second thought. It was really only due to a desperate grasp at finding normalcy that he was there in the first place and not snoozing in the medical bay after a lot of fancy talking and promises he probably wouldn't be able to keep.

"About an hour," Corin answered from the left. "Already cruised right past the welcome wagon. Guess they remember this old hunk of scrap, after all."

"It hasn't been that long," James replied. It had been maybe two years, which on the outer planets seemed to pass like a day when there was nothing better to do than get in trouble and scrape by. He imagined she could see the first glimpses of Verona already, the small moons orbiting the planet and serving to guide her toward the port. The thought didn't warm James much.

Home was a place James would rather not be, but given their situation, it was the only place safe enough to hide out, at least until Michael was back on his feet and the heat had died down a little. It was a place of secrets and regrets and a lot of things that were a whole lot simpler to avoid.

"Did you call ahead and let her know you're coming?" Corin asked, ever tactful.

"I'm not gonna use an open channel without my port." It was as good an excuse as any; if Corin pushed the topic, James would remind her Lyra was capable of monitoring open feeds, even if she probably had much better things to do than scan in hopes of tracking them down. In truth, it was simply easier to show up and catch the hell he was due, without giving Anika time to arrange a proper greeting party.

Corin fell quiet, letting James drink in the low hum of the engine and equipment around them. The closer they got, the sooner it was before he was face-to-face with the other woman—other than Lyra—who seemed to run his life without even laying a finger on him, and it was more than a little unsettling. At least Anika was unlikely to kill someone, unless her disposition had changed in the last couple years.

"Did you tell your *boyfriend*?" Corin asked, drawing a sigh from deep in James's chest. "You know, eventually, you're going to have to tell him what he's gotten himself into."

James's skin crawled thinking about explaining the situation to him, so it was easier to focus on the part that didn't matter. "He's not my boyfriend yet."

"*Yet.*" Corin laughed, and James got the distinct impression she was rolling her eyes. "Come on, we both know the only reason you didn't leave his ass back in the sand was because you're sweet on him."

"It's complicated."

She snorted. "Astrophysics is complicated. This is just like when—"

"Don't you dare say his name." James grimaced at the thought, tasting blood in his mouth before realizing he'd bitten his own tongue. "And it's not. Michael's... He's a good person. I kidnapped him, and he fixed everything."

She didn't answer at first, but when she did, James's ears burned with shame. "You're a good man, too, James. Just got a different kind of good in you."

"He's not one of us." James was digging for excuses more for himself than her, resisting the urge to do more than imply Michael was better than all of them.

"He could be. Band of misfits, half of us wanted for something. He fits right in."

The only thing standing in the way of admitting they had more in common now was how much James didn't want to ruin him, and like it or not, when you run with broken people, your turn comes up sooner or later. "He ain't got blood on his hands. I'd like to keep him that way."

The instrument panel coming to life in a series of beeps and clicks cut off any response she had, which was for the better really. "Welcome home, James..." Corin said, clicking on the ship intercom. "Ten minutes till we dock in Verona; get your shit together."

Twelve: Anika

CORIN LED JAMES down the gangway, as subtly as she could, both of them aware the last thing Anika needed to see was that James couldn't. Still, the fist in the small of his back was a little uncalled for when she signaled him to stop.

"James Marks." The familiar voice drove ice through James's veins, but he forced a smile anyway. "I was starting to wonder if you'd ever show your face in the Queendom again."

Forcing his smile even wider, James put on all the airs he could manage in his less-than-presentable state. He'd managed to put a nice shirt on, despite pulling the fresh wound, but Corin impressed how—in her words—disgusting his face looked. "Anika, darling. As though I could stay away too long."

Anika made a small sound of approval, but it was hard to tell how much of James's bullshit she ever bought. "Just the usual rabble?"

"Lost two 'bout a year back. There's a new one, our engineer. Name's Michael."

Corin cleared her throat. "Edge and Razor are being cleared for weapons. Michael's laid up in the medbay— took an old-fashioned bullet to the chest."

"So he's a dead man?" Anika laughed, and James held back the urge to jump to his defense. This particular moment was one best to left to someone with no emotional investment.

"No. We got him patched up. James too." Corin paused as if waiting for Anika to comment, James could feel her eyes on him, sizing him up to see how bad off the crew was to turn to her for safe harbor. "We only need a place to stay for a couple weeks."

"I see." Anika's hand rested on James's shoulder for a moment, and then traced up to the ragged opening where the doctors had tried to fix his port. "You're pretty bad off. How much heat are we talking about, *James*?"

Holding steady, with great difficulty, against the urge to simply go back to the ship and leave, James answered. "Three with a price on their head. But we can manage with the Corporate heat. We're dealing with a bigger fish."

"Lyra?" Anika asked without hesitation, as though it couldn't possibly be anyone else.

"She tried to kill me. My crew's in danger." James knew there was no swaying her; the decision was already made one way or the other. It was the reason she'd been ruling the civilized portion of the planet for over a decade. "If you want me to, I'll beg. Give us a chance. Please?"

"For old time's sake?" Anika laughed again, a sound that once brought to mind tinkling glass and china, now feeling more like the scream of metal on metal. "Oh, James, honey, you are still trying after all these years? I told you last time you came limping back here that woman was going to get you killed one day. Why delay the inevitable?"

"It's not about me," James growled back, feeling a tremor through his hands. "She's lost her mind. I'm just one of a hundred bugs she'll squash."

"I see." Anika's heels clattered against the floor, and James could see her in his mind as she was the last time he left: regal, beautiful, red hair pinned up against her head as she looked down at him with the most intense green eyes he'd ever seen. "And *you* are going to fix the problem?"

"Someone has to," James replied, hearing Corin swallow back a lump in her throat beside him. "I know the Queendom won't move against her, but you know as well as I do that as long as she has a stranglehold on the scavs, your people won't be able to get a foot in the door." Money, at least, was a language she was fluent in.

Anika walked away then, no doubt checking over the crew herself; a dramatic pronouncement was coming after all. "We'll talk," she spoke firmly, and James felt Corin's hand on his back again. "You know my palace always has room for the SIO's crew."

"Thank you for your generosity, Queen Anika," Corin said, her voice betraying a touch of a bitter tongue.

"Of course," Anika purred. "Fetch this *engineer*; he may need more *adequate* medical attention than those butchers who keep after scavs."

James was escorted to the room he'd occupied years before, a long walk into the palace proper and up a flight of stairs, down a long corridor on the second floor of her disgustingly large home.

Corin lingered behind with him after the palace guard left and guided James to the bed. "That was...expected," she said. "Your room hasn't changed at all."

"Good," James said, moving to look around and seeing only darkness. "We'll be safe here."

"Yeah, until you piss her off."

"I won't piss her off. Just—just make sure they bring Michael here after they're done with him? Please?"

She grumbled and answered, "Are you sure that's a good idea? Sharing a bed? *Here*?"

"It's been six years since...since she had a right to say who I couldn't share a bed with." The bitterness seeped through James now that he wasn't under Anika's judgmental gaze. "If she asks, he's working on my implant."

"Right. Of course. I agree, spineless is definitely the way to go in this instance," she groused, but James could hear the serious tone underneath her snark.

"Make it happen, please. For me?"

JAMES HEARD MICHAEL'S voice before he was even in the room, chatting idly, as he was brought down the hall, about how *amazingly up-to-date* the medical facilities were and how impressed he was at the level of tech he'd seen. It was a good start at least. Anika always prided herself in having the best of everything.

"Little blonde said to bring him up to you," a deep voice said after James heard the door open. "I take it this was Captain's orders?"

"That's right," James answered, trying to look as though he'd been interrupted in his thinking and not idly dozing. "Keeping watch over him until he can take a peek at my neural implant."

"Right, well—" the voice said, quickly cut off by Michael's voice.

"They have *nanobots*, James! Fucking *nanobots*!" he squealed excitedly. "I hurt like hell, but I walked all the way up the stairs!"

"Sort of," the voice corrected. "You need to get some rest; doctor's orders, okay?"

"Sure thing, Reg," Michael called back, and the bed barely shifted under his light weight. "Promise, no walking around unless I have to; it feels so good to be out of bed for a minute."

"Right..." Reg answered, closing the door without further comment.

James felt Michael's arm gingerly snake around him, and then he leaned into James's good side with his bad side making only a slightly pained sound. "Your home is *fantastic*! I can't believe you could be living like this and actually want to be on that cramped little ship all the time."

"It's complicated," James answered simply enough, adding, "I'm not exactly the high life kind of guy."

Michael nodded against James's shoulder, and then James was aware of a smooth hand on his chin, guiding him into a soft, unexpected kiss. Michael's skin felt perfect against his stubble, and the simple pleasure of his touch eased James's nerves far more than he'd ever admit. "I met the Queen," he said, breaking the kiss. "She seems kind."

"Anika is..." James sighed. "She's something."

The door opened again, and James didn't need to hear her voice to know who had come to call. "Only something?" Anika said in a cool tone. "That's no way to talk about your wife."

The calm that Michael had given James shattered when the touch moved away. That would be exactly why James didn't want to tell him, one of many secrets tucked away, but one that increasingly seemed relevant. James muttered, "You're not my wife anymore, Anika. It's been years since you were."

"Funny, coming from the man who, ten years ago, jumped at the chance to be my king." She laughed, stepping closer as the door closed behind her.

"James?" Michael said in a small, sad voice. He was confused; anyone would be, in his situation. "What is going on here?"

"Oh, do explain our little *situation*, James. It's been far too long since I've seen you try to weasel your way out of something."

It wasn't an easy thing to explain, least of all when she was staring James down—caught with Michael, no less. It wasn't the first time she'd put him in that kind of position, and he could only hope Michael would understand. "You needed me as much as I needed you, Anika. Don't pretend there was ever a romance between us. I was convenient in a time when the Queendom needed someone to lull them into a sense of security about their Queen and the royal bloodline"

"You wound me, James," Anika replied. James could feel her close enough to touch, to taste her flowery perfume, and the sheer sense of her made him shiver. "Yet, you can't say I wasn't a good wife..."

"You're a wife in title only." James reached out to Michael, feeling him freeze beside him when James placed a hand on his arm. "And I'm not the king."

She scoffed. James knew her eyes were burning down at him and he could only imagine how Michael felt. "No, I imagine not. Your son will bear the title when my time is done."

Michael drew in a deep breath, ending with a pained gulp. "You have a son?"

"And a daughter," James added, with as little emotion as he could muster. "They don't know me."

"Of course, they don't, James. You always have been, and always will be, thieving scav trash with a taste for..." She trailed off, no doubt bearing down on Michael with those cold green eyes. "Well, typically not this particular flavor of boys, but I suppose you've probably run out of rough trade by now."

James shook his head and sighed. "Are you done, Anika? If you're here to humiliate me, I think you've made your point." There was no sense in denying any of it; she hadn't told a lie, no matter how rotten it sounded in her mouth.

"No, I thought you should know that Tyrian is due home tomorrow, and I'm sure he'd love to be regaled with tales of your adventures." She sighed, but moved away toward the door.

The mention of his son was conflicting at best. He'd been starting his tutoring when James left, and he realized Tyrian would probably be almost eleven now. "I don't want him to see me like this."

"Of course, you don't. How long do you think you could pretend to not be blind as a bat? I'll send a man up in the morning."

Unexpectedly, Michael jumped in with a bold, firm tone. "No. I'll be taking care of him."

From anyone else, James would have shrugged it off, but from Michael, he realized it was far more than wanting to prove he could fix the damage. He was still on James's side. He understood. James cleared his throat. "I think we've got this one. But thank you, Queen Anika, for the gracious offer."

"Certainly, husband," she replied with an icy drip to her voice. "Careful you don't *kill* this one. He seems nice."

Michael's hand curled at James's side, and his nails worried at the bandage there, but Michael held his tongue as long as James did. When she was gone, Michael let out a held breath, and James leaned gingerly into him. "I'm sorry," he muttered. "I said it was complicated."

"No…I understand, I think."

"She was different then, not so cold. She needed someone." As hard as he tried, James couldn't make it sound any better than what it was. "I needed the protection she gave me, and in return, I gave her the things she couldn't get on her own."

"Children," Michael muttered breathlessly. "You have children."

"By blood only. They were never supposed to see me as more than a *friend* of the family. I don't think they ever will."

Michael's body relaxed slightly, leaning into James as much as his remaining wounds would allow. "Are we safe here?"

James turned his head, searching for Michael's mouth but only finding dirty hair under his lips. It would do. "You're safe," James murmured. "She doesn't really like me much."

Michael chuckled, and for the first time since getting shot, James didn't hear the telltale wheeze of pain. "I got that impression. But, in her defense, you kind of are thieving scav trash."

James smiled reflexively and added, "And I do have a taste for men…well, one man who currently happens to be on the mend." It felt right, despite the circumstance, to have Michael there with him. He was pretty sure he knew, then and there, the answer to Corin's question back in the medical center.

"How about first we focus on fixing you, and then we'll deal with that other thing." James felt Michael's lips press against his shirt and nodded into him.

"Fair enough."

Thirteen: Verona

THEY RESTED WELL into the night, listening to the din of the palace die down. Michael told James about the nanobots and how they were repairing the damaged tissue from the inside out, about how nanobot tech had been mostly abandoned by corporations as they interfered with most tech. Michael explained why he was so excited and how the nanobots were healing him from the inside out in terms that James actually understood, even if it felt a little patronizing. In a lot of ways, James was pretty sure Michael wanted him to worry less about what had happened.

The truth was it didn't matter. They were alive and they were together. After the week they'd been through, it was good enough. They had a goal and somewhere safe to work out the rough parts.

"Can I take a look at your port?" Michael asked, well after the city chime had rung midnight.

"I don't want you to strain yourself," James answered. "I can wait."

Michael grumbled, "I hate you, you know that? It's okay to want this fixed. You're hardly an outlaw when you can't even make it across the room without tripping over something."

"Are you kidding? I make blindness cool again," James shot back, smiling reflexively. "I'll be the best visually impaired scav ever."

James felt Michael move beside him, reaching, and hoped it wasn't for his tools. Unfortunately for James's libido, he was wrong. "We're going to have to sit up," Michael said, voice dropping into a hollow groan as he slowly pulled himself upright. "On the edge of the bed."

"You realize there are at least four better things we could be doing in bed right now," James muttered, sitting up anyway and sliding to the edge of the bed with the guidance of Michael's hands against his side and back.

James didn't have to see Michael to know he was frowning as he slid up behind James. He felt the increasingly familiar buzz of electricity behind his ear again, gentle at first, but then a painful red heat radiated outward. "Let me know if it hurts too much," Michael whispered, the sensation coupled with a sudden sharp piercing pain drilling into his port.

James swore under his breath but tried not to think about the strange sensation of Michael's probing. "You know, I like the idea of you inside me, but this is *definitely* not what I had in mind."

"Trust me," Michael murmured, brushing a kiss on James's shoulder as the probe in his head twisted, winding and catching on something deep in his skull. "Okay, the good news is nothing *appears* to be disconnected. I'm running a diagnostic now."

A thin wire unraveled from the pulsing hot point, brushing against James's neck as he heard the soft *click* of Michael plugging it into his pad. James held his breath, waiting for the flash of numbers and letters that didn't come. "I...I don't see it." James could sense the higher brain functions kicking in, though, and that alone was reassuring. Over the years, he'd gotten used to the constant background activities to the point where he never knew when he was passively scanning until something flashed up into his vision on the HUD. Not having it was lonely and quiet.

"It's okay," Michael whispered, the softness of his voice unexpected. "I'm working on it." His arm wrapped around James's waist, and Michael's forehead pressed on the back of his shirt as they waited. Michael's skilled fingers slid along James's profile, following the squareness of his unshaven jaw to his ear, and then lingered around the edge of the port, exploring the small metal ring where it sank into the skin behind his ear.

"How bad is it? Really?" James had touched it himself, but all he could feel was smooth metal and ragged skin.

Michael took a deep breath, his body hitching with a pang of pain, but answered, "It's bad." His datapad let out a soft beep, and then a low whine as the program continued. "The port itself is damaged...on the inside."

"Right." James said, knowing full well what it would require to fix. "So, I'm fucked?"

"I didn't say that." Michael withdrew the probe slowly, an unexpected moan escaping James's throat as it tingled through his nervous system in a way that was completely unfair to his body. "I can force your optics back online, I think."

"Okay..." James said. The curious lilt to Michael's voice worried him. "What's the catch?"

The thin cord tickled against James's neck as Michael rewound it, taking his time to answer. Finally, Michael said, "That's all I'll be able to fix without a functioning workshop or until I'm really back on my feet."

With a low *zip*, the heat stopped, and James let out a relieved sigh. "I guess that's better than nothing at all, right?"

Michael hesitated, and James could feel Michael once more frozen against his back, one hand lingering on the damaged port. "It'll hurt. Probably a lot."

"Everything does." James leaned back into him, letting him know it was okay; it was what it was. Michael surprised him again and strained to press a kiss against the hole in his head. It was strange, but James remembered back to Terro 9—his lips on Michael's scar, the look on his face when James showed him it didn't bother him at all. "I can talk to Anika's men. I'm sure they can—"

"No," Michael said firmly, the warm lips once more gone, followed again by the hot electric current. "I can do this."

James understood what Michael really meant was that he *had* to do it. It's what he would have felt in Michael's place. It wasn't even a matter of pride, just a matter of what was right. "Do what you gotta do."

"Right..." Michael whispered and then drew a deep breath.

And then there was nothing.

MICHAEL TRIED, AND if James had thought they had any chance of succeeding, he would have at least pretended the sharp pain drilling through his skull had yielded positive results. Unfortunately, when Michael finally laid down his tools with a frustrated, strained sigh, James felt blindly for his hand and grasped it tightly. "I'm sorry," Michael said, voice shaking with an obvious hitch in his breath. "I... That should have worked. I'm sorry. I'm so stupid."

"Stop it," James chided, gripping tighter around Michael's fingers. He pulled Michael's knuckles to his lips and kissed them. "It was a long shot. You'll fix it next time."

"No," Michael said and leaned his head against James's shoulder. "No, you can get Anika's people to do it. I...I can't."

It was a blow to him; James got that right away, but he'd always more or less believed that you can't really call something a failure until someone was dead. "Nah, 'fraid I can't do that." James wrapped an arm over Michael's shoulder, feeling his body relax under his weight. "If anyone's gonna cause me that much fucking pain, I choose you."

"I don't know."

James sighed and pushed to his feet, not surprised when Michael rose up under his arm with a guiding hand against his back. "Let's go out on the balcony. I need some air that doesn't smell like fried electronics."

Michael hesitated but didn't say a word as he guided James across the familiar floor. Michael opened the door and drew in a deep breath. James could recall what he must be seeing from memory; sure, it had probably changed a little since the last time he had been there, but Verona was always a sight to be seen.

"Beautiful, isn't it?" James asked, taking the last unsteady steps forward until his hands found the balcony railing. "Have you ever seen anything like it?"

James could hear the Queendom below, humming with energy, and smell the silicone smoke clinging to the air. There weren't many real cities on the outer planets, too few resources to go around and barely enough people to set up a small community and make it work with what little they had. The Queendom had no such problems. The soil was rich, the climate temperate, and the sky soft blue with fertile rains. Over the years, the population had grown so fast that, when Anika took over, one of the first orders she gave was restricting the number of folks allowed to live within Verona and the sister city, Scion. It had become a haven for mercs and scavs; there was enough cash flowing through the cities that business usually ran smooth for the few who didn't already have contracts with a benefactor like Lyra. Outside the gates of the cities were small, mostly lawless villages where anyone who didn't start shit was welcome to bed down if you were willing to risk the chance a merc might call in your number.

"No," Michael said and stepped up to James's side, leaning into him. Corporate Space was nothing but industry, single buildings the size of all of Verona, if not larger, with no windows to look out at the scorched skies. The view between the docks and the palace wasn't much to see—a lot of ships and staff—but from up in the raised palace you really could get a sense of the best things narrowly within your grasp. "It's... Is this real?"

James laughed; the first time he'd seen the view, he'd thought the same thing. It reminded him too much of the story of Eden to actually be a real place. "Do you see the tree with the little pink berries?" He gestured vaguely in the direction where it should be, its growth spilling over the balcony railing naturally.

"What are they?" Michael murmured, shifting away again.

"Pick some; they're the best. I'll have to ask Tyrian what they're called. I don't remember." At the mention of James's son's name, Michael sighed but didn't say a word.

James was acutely aware of how much he missed being able to see Michael's generally annoyed face and get a sense of what was going on in his head, at least the stuff he could actually understand. James listened for the snapping of thin branches and the rustle of leaves before asking: "You gonna be okay?"

"Yeah, I'm getting them," Michael answered.

"Not what I mean," James replied, closing his eyes with the frustration. "It's been a pretty fucked-up situation since back at Peach. I mean...how're you holding up?"

Michael didn't answer right away. James heard a small grunt of effort and then quick footsteps coming back to where he stood. "I'm here," Michael answered. "I'm more worried about fixing you."

"I'm fine. Seriously, Michael. Do you even know how much shit you're in right now?"

Michael sighed loudly. "Peach wants me dead. Your boss almost killed me. I'm pretty sure your neural interface chip is dead." His voice started as a droll monotone that perked up after a short pause and a soft groan of delight. "Oh wow...these are amazing."

James understood; things had pretty much hit the level of fucked so it was hard to think about it at all at once. One problem at a time was a little less taxing. "They are," he answered, leaning against Michael. "I've got to give it to Anika—she knows how to wring the best out of life."

"You sound like you don't like it much." Michael's knuckles stroked up James's arm, and then he pressed a berry against James's lips.

It tasted as good as he remembered, sweet and just a little tart, not like anything he'd found on any other planet. "Imagine a life where everything was handed to you and the worst thing that ever happened was accidentally insulting the wrong person at a party. That's pretty much life in the palace. Sure, nothing bad really happens, but that's because nothing really happens in general."

"Sounds like a better version of the Corporate dream." Michael offered him another berry, and James let his lips linger on Michael's fingertips until he pulled them away. "So you got bored? Of all this?"

James shook his head. It was more complicated than that, more than he could really explain to someone who never really knew what it was to be free. "I saw it for what it was. There are good people here, a hell of a lot of them, but they're docile. May as well be animals waiting for slaughter."

"You're worried about an attack?"

"Not really." Lyra's people were about the only group James had heard of that could possibly have the manpower to launch any sort of attack, and it'd be cutting their own throats to do it; not that he'd put it past Lyra after what'd happened. "I was worried I'd end up like them."

Michael's hand rested on James's elbow for a long moment as he ate the berries he'd picked, making several small pleased noises. "Am I going with you when your crew leaves?"

James didn't want Michael to know how badly he hoped he would stay with them; it wasn't exactly like he could offer more than the wealth Verona had, and given his background, Anika would welcome Michael to stay without even thinking about it. "If you want to, you're welcome. I'm sure Anika can be swayed to let someone with your skill and knowledge stay here."

"Do you want me to stay here?" Michael whispered, fingers gently squeezing James's elbow.

It wasn't a fair question, not at all. "Ain't my place to tell you what to do."

"That's not what I asked." Michael leaned into James then, the corner of his glasses digging into James's arm.

James put an arm around him, hearing the small pained draw of breath it drew out. "No. No, it's not. Come on. We should get some sleep before tomorrow."

Fourteen: Trying

MORNING SUN WARMED James's skin as he woke. They'd left the balcony doors open all night to let in the fresh air that held little chill, and the fragrant blossoms outside wafted into the small room. At some point in the night Michael's arm had come to rest on James's belly, and he realized Michael was lying on his wounded side. Apparently the tech was working its magic well enough. James rolled toward him, feeling Michael's bare chest against his and the cadence of his soft sleep breaths. With a tug of pain from his side, James reached out and stroked his fingers through Michael's hair. He could picture him easily, that innocent face blank, save for a sweet smile curling his lips.

Michael stirred and let out a soft groan, nuzzling closer with the gentle urging of James's touch. He buried his head in James's shoulder, and James answered with a kiss against Michael's forehead. He'd gone to bed frustrated; James wouldn't tell him what to do. Truth was, James hoped when the time came the choice would be obvious—either he'd want to stay or go. "Morning, sunshine," James murmured, finding Michael's brow with his lips.

Michael groaned, and his arm squeezed tight around James. When the pain drew out a gasp, he lifted it away immediately. "Shit— Sorry."

"It's okay; put it back."

Michael hesitated, and when he reached out again, his fingers traced idly along James's hip and then along the curve of his ass. "I'll get your meds."

"No." James brushed his fingers through Michael's hair again, and then followed his neck down to his shoulder. "I'm okay for now." It wasn't really a lie; he could hold it together a little longer, though he was sore— all part of the fun of getting shot. "Stay right here."

Michael chuckled, and his lips pressed against James's shoulder and then his throat. "*Right* here?" he asked coyly, his wandering hand suddenly under the light blanket, which had drifted down to their hips, cupping over James's cock. "Or maybe here?"

James couldn't resist smiling, but he probably could have resisted pressing back against that touch. It was worth the tug of pain that came with it. "Dealer's choice."

"You're terrible." Michael laughed again, nipping James's shoulder blade.

James's mouth shot off without thinking. "You love it." For a moment, Michael didn't speak, didn't even move, and James was pretty sure he'd said something Michael didn't want to hear.

Then Michael leaned into him, guiding him down onto his back on the soft bed, and kissed him. "I think I do." He sighed, resting his head on James's shoulder as his fingers left the zone of lust and idly trailed over James's firm belly.

Maybe it was a good night's sleep in a soft bed, maybe it was the way he said it so easily, but when James dug up against him, finding Michael's lips to kiss him again and then again, it was easy to say the words that had been lingering since their brush with death. "I think I do too."

For another drawn moment Michael was silent again, dragging heavy thoughtful breaths against James's ear. Then he whispered, "You're the first person who's ever made me feel like I'm more than just another tech geek."

"Because you are." James groped for the hand hovering below his navel and wrapped his fingers over Michael's. "You see me," James said. The words were hard to sort in his head, and he wasn't sure how to explain what it meant to have someone see the whole picture. "I'm not only a scav, or a thief, or the captain."

Michael's wrist turned, and then he cupped James's hand and entwined their fingers. "You're not *only* anything, James." James didn't need to see his face to know he was sincere. Michael kissed him again, and then dared to lean his chest against James's good side. "I want to be with you."

James's guts knotted in a weird meeting of pain, desire, and affection. Yet again, he was at a loss for words at Michael's honesty. Then his lips kissed behind James's left ear against the damaged port there, lingering as he nuzzled against his face. Michael shifted, pushing up and bracing himself under James's arms as he leaned over his chest. "Don't hurt yourself," James said quickly, reaching up to him with a wince of his own pain. "You're healing."

"James..." Michael said, and James heard the ripping of tape before he lifted James's hand to his chest, pressing his palm against the spot that had nearly been a death wound the last time he'd seen it. "Feel."

James held his hand there, giving himself time to absorb the fact he couldn't even feel the stitching where the doctors had closed Michael up. The skin was hot to the touch, vibrating strangely against his palm. The only evidence Michael had been on death's door was a scar no larger than James's thumbnail. "Shit..."

"I haven't felt this good since...since a long time ago."

"I need to get me some of those nanobots." James chuckled, sucking in another pained breath with the pull of his own wound. "You know, if they wouldn't destroy my tech."

"Let me take care of you," Michael said, an earnest lilt to his voice. "Please, James. You'd do the same for me."

It wasn't the first time someone had offered to help him through rough times, but every time came with some kind of expectation attached. That said, James trusted him probably more than he'd trusted anyone in a long time, even his own crew, mostly because Michael trusted him when he had every damn reason not to. "Yeah," James answered as smoothly as he could manage in his pained state. "Sure."

It seemed to be enough. Michael's face softened against his cheek before Michael kissed him again. Michael's lips touched on his, his jaw, his throat, and then down his scarred chest. Without his sight, James found it easy to become overly sensitive, especially when Michael's touch was fairly new to him, and the brush of his lips against James's belly made him groan. "Michael..." he whispered, not even sure why.

Michael didn't stop. His kisses lingered with small flashes of his tongue across James's skin down to his thigh. Michael crouched between James's legs, and the anticipation knotted in his guts as fingers squeezed his thighs on each side, skin and flesh on the left and the intersection of metal and sinew on the right. "I'd tell you I think you're handsome," Michael said softly, letting out a soft laugh, "but I think you'd agree with me."

Only as Michael's touch lingered on the scarring, where the leg became more machine than man, did James realize fully what Michael was talking about before. There were some things most people never got to see, some things even people James ended up in bed with never saw, and that was one of them. It was more personal than his cock, more personal than even the battle scars written across his torso to remind him what brand of fresh hell he'd been through just living. And now Michael was looking at it, touching it, not afraid of it or disgusted. "Ignore my metal," James muttered, a warm flush washing over his chest and cheeks. "That's what I do."

"I don't want to ignore it," Michael protested, and for a moment, James considered the lingering touch that had first made him take notice of Michael way back on some godforsaken sun-bleached shithole. After a long moment, that touch became a soft press of his lips. "It's part of you."

"It's an eyesore." And really, it was. Metal and fastened-down wires with a flexible enough knee that could put more spring than James really liked in his step. It wasn't there to look pretty; it was functional, and from time to time, pretty fucking cool, but not the sort of thing your average rake would take pride in.

Michael's lips admired the jagged scars of long-healed flesh, where the muscle had been ripped clean off the bone. Then, his kisses pushed lower. James couldn't feel it, there was no synthetic skin covering, and the limited sensations provided by his neural implant had gone offline when he'd lost everything else in his head, but James knew it was what he had to be doing. Admiring the leg's craftsmanship, those tiny little tinkerer's fingers searching out every plane and wire he could find. "It's beautiful," Michael murmured in reply, reaching to James's left leg to squeeze above the knee. "People write them off as another piece of simple equipment, nothing high tech with lines of code and intricate chips, but that's what makes them so interesting. The kind of thing you forget exists and changes people's lives...tech that kind of blends into the background like...well, like you."

"You callin' me simple?" James smiled, listening to Michael's reverent words as he was surely working his way down to the slab of light metal that approximated a foot well enough to fit in James's old boots.

Michael laughed and tapped his fingers on the metal. "No, no. You're an asshole, but not simple. You want everyone to think that's what you are. You blend in, you lie, you do everything you can to look like you're like everyone else when you're...well..." He laughed a little louder, the sound almost strange coming from down around James's knees. "You're something else."

"That's what they tell me." The reply rolled off James's tongue even as his mind worked over what Michael was telling him, what he was really saying and how genuine it all sounded. Back in the days before tech was commonplace, people liked to use words like *augmented*. There was even a whole movement sponsored by the first Corporate overlords toward what they liked to call *transhumanism,* a better life through augmentation of any kind they could dream up. Now it was the way things were; folks with some sort of tech in them were the majority. "Usually before I end up in a fistfight."

Michael stopped and pulled down on his metal foot, examining it as he bent the ankle joint full circle. "Fascinating."

"What, that I've had my ass kicked more than a few times?"

"No. Stop that." James could hear the frown and furrowed brows in Michael's voice, but then his weight shifted on the bed and he was moving closer again—kissing the old scars along James's thigh once more.

James let him explore, the knot of anticipation in his gut coiling and uncoiling again as Michael traced long lines between lingering caresses. "Glad you like it. I usually don't feel exactly comfortable when people see me like this." It was an honest enough admission, though not nearly so much *don't like* as *absolutely refuse to allow*.

"You're vulnerable now," Michael said in that same soft, curiously tender voice. "Guy like you doesn't want anyone to know you're not quite as badass as you seem."

"I am *just* as badass as I seem." James grinned, knowing full well Michael would call him on his shit. "You haven't had a chance to see me properly use my skills."

"What? Lying? Talking your way out of a fight? Standing up to someone who could kill you as easy as look at you?" Okay, so maybe he had a point. Things had gotten more than a little interesting in the last week or so. "Saving someone's life? Turning down a *lot* of money—"

James cut him off before he could get really sappy. "All right, I get it. I get it."

"You're not a fighter. You don't want to hurt people in a job where sometimes people have to get hurt." Michael's voice softened, and the gentle kisses gradually rose to tease at the slope of James's belly, drawing out another throaty groan. "It's why I'm still here." Michael paused, and James felt his small hands hesitantly caressing his inner thighs. "And why I don't want to be anywhere else."

James knew there were words, something he probably should have said in that moment, but whatever they were, it was gone when Michael's lips brushed against his cock. He didn't only kiss that tender skin; he caressed it, the tip of his tongue tasting over the crown and then down one side until he was eagerly licking and nuzzling against the root of James's manhood. James moaned softly, holding back the urge to push against the sensation for his side's sake more than anything else.

Michael lingered, adoring every inch of flesh tentatively at first and then with that same eager desire until he was nursing at the head of James's cock, drawing slowly as his tongue coaxed him up to full strength. "Mmmm..." Michael groaned as he took James's manhood down the length of his tongue, swallowing when it brushed against the back of his throat and then a little deeper.

"Fuck..." James moaned, the word drawing out of his aching chest and filling the room. It wasn't fair how easily such a little man could have someone, supposedly strong, coming undone. James had tangled with the biggest bastards he'd ever known in *every* possible way, and it took a gentle little man like Michael to find the one who knew exactly where to play those well-kept hands and hungry tongue. "Feels good..."

Michael grunted, swallowing again as he breathed heavily through his nose. One hand again caressed James's right thigh, darting over that crease where metal met skin as the other stroked just as lovingly over his balls and squeezed enough to make James's breath catch. Michael made a low, groaning noise in the back of his throat that rattled down his cock to his very core.

James moved to sit up then, to reach for Michael, but a strong stitch of shooting pain put him flat on his back again. Another great reminder of his current limitations, as if it wasn't frustrating enough to be unable to see the look on Michael's face as he slowly withdrew and then took James's cock between his warm lips. "Michael..." James breathed, reaching down until he could barely ruffle his fingertips in Michael's sweaty blond hair. "Fuck, Michael..."

The gentle squeeze on James's balls became a single-minded stroke of Michael's thumb, softness drawing over tender skin as he continued to drive his tongue and throat against James's cock. When he tipped over the edge, James's fists balled in the blankets, and he cried out loud enough to no doubt rouse the room beside theirs. Michael only groaned around his cock, swallowing fast and hard until James was a whimpering, mewling mess. Then, he lifted up with a chuckle and pressed wet kisses against James's thigh. "Mm-hmm, definitely sexy."

"Not fair! You...you just sucked my dick." James managed a weak laugh that left him aching despite the postorgasm buzz. "Pretty sure everyone looks better after they get off."

Michael shifted again, curling onto the opposite side between James's bandaged wound and the edge of the large bed. James could feel Michael's arousal butting hard against his thigh and let the guilt linger for a while before offering, "I should...I mean, I could—"

"Don't," Michael said firmly, tracing lines around the bandage taped down against James's skin. "I'm good. I'll go get your meds."

"Please." James reached out for him again, his wound pulling painfully as he ran his fingers over Michael's face, realizing at some point in the last minute Michael had already put on his glasses as James's fingers knocked them askew. "I want to try."

Michael took James by the hand as he threaded his fingers through Michael's fine hair and followed it down to his ear, once more joining their fingers together. "James. I'm telling you as your technician and not your...well, whatever. It'll hurt you *far* more than I'll enjoy it."

"Damn it," James swore under his breath and slammed his free hand against the mattress. "Don't treat me like I'm helpless here! I dragged myself four *fucking* kilometers with a bleeding stump of a leg, okay? I can cope with a little pain."

Michael sighed, but it didn't sound frustrated, so much as tender. "I know, James. I know you're not weak. I don't want you to hurt any more than you have to. I can wait. Believe me, I've spent a *long time* with myself."

It was frustrating, infuriating even, to not have that little normalcy. "You're not alone, Michael. I don't want you to feel you have to act like y'are."

"I want to try something," Michael murmured against his ear and then unexpectedly shifted his hips again. "Just...stay where you are, okay? Don't move."

"What—" James started, and then stopped midthought, realizing exactly what Michael was doing. Michael rocked his hips, definitely purposeful, and pushed his cock along the old scars ringing James's thigh. Michael gasped, a soft needy sound in the quiet room, and James realized if it had been anyone else it would have made things feel pretty fucking weird, but with Michael, it made a perverse kind of sense. The man had spent most of his life around technology: picking it apart, building it from parts and the lines of code in his head, creating tech, destroying tech, discovering tech. It only made sense that he might want to fuck it.

At least James figured that's what was going through Michael's head as the quick jerk of his hips became all the more obvious. Michael gasped against his ear and then moaned again, lowering his head to kiss James on the neck as he felt his Michael's palm stroking over his length, guiding it against his leg—against skin, and then warm metal.

"Gonna come for me?" James asked, smiling reflexively at the strange sensation as wetness began to smear across the ragged cleft. "C'mon, Michael, I know you want to. Go ahead and let go."

Michael whimpered, and James could feel the heat of him blushing when he buried his head in the crook of James's neck. He might be ashamed, James figured; a touch of kink was the sort of thing he probably thought nobody would ever know about him. "It's okay," James said, softening his voice as he squeezed his hand tighter. "I get it."

"D-don't..." Michael stammered, his breath hitching as his hips slowed, favoring more powerful strokes that rattled his body against James's solid frame, gentle, but eager.

"Please."

That word seemed to be the key. Michael sighed and then gasped, letting it out as a hollow moan against James's shoulder as he stroked sticky heat against his thigh, digging the tip of his cock against the imperfect seam until the final spasms left him sucking a deep breath and flushed hot. "James..." he whimpered, pressing a hard kiss on his shoulder. "I..."

James knew it was his turn to be tough. "Don't," he answered the unspoken worry, feeling the creases in Michael's face as he nuzzled into James's shoulder. "It's good. You're good."

Michael rolled away, keeping their hands tightly clasped against his belly, and then rough wadded toweling wiped over James's skin, cleaning away the evidence of his lust. A long silence passed between them, but right when James thought Michael understood what he was saying, Michael continued, "I swear, I've— I mean, I never would—"

James laughed, instantly regretting it not so much for the fact that he knew it would upset Michael in his moment of awkward apologetics, but rather for the rip of pain it sent through his guts. "You're a tech perv; it's fine. I'm, uh, kind of not one to judge. I mean, half man, half machine. I'm a fucking freak compared to what you see in Corporate Space."

"You're not a freak," Michael answered firmly, and for a moment James could imagine that angry little man face he hadn't seen since back before Lyra had shot them. He continued, "Your enhancements—"

James cut him off, mostly because it'd be what he already said with his kindness and with his desire. "They are what they are. I'm just glad you don't hate them. Or me."

Michael was silent, no doubt stewing on James's words, and then let out a frustrated sigh. "I hate you. Still. I mean, you're clearly a jerk."

"Nah, guys like you don't go for jerks. I'm really more of a playful miscreant."

"Guys like you don't know what *miscreant* means."

The laugh was reflexive this time and came with pain not only across James's abdomen, but with a sharp jab in his shoulder that radiated fresh warmth. The little bastard had injected him without warning. "Damn it, Michael, warn me when you do that!"

"I was getting tired of you refusing to take your pain meds," Michael answered in a simple, clipped retort. "You need it if you're gonna keep laughing like an idiot."

"Well, if you weren't so damn funny…"

DAYTIME CAME WITH responsibilities and a palace that was buzzing with activity. James could feel Corin's stare digging knives into him when she slammed open the door to his room as he talked Michael through the delicate art of helping him put on a pair of clean pants. "James! Do you have any idea what I had to go through to get these?"

James looked up toward the sound of her voice and smiled. He had plenty of idea what it took to get clothes for someone else on a planet that preferred credits and treated those with more access to gold like they had to get blood on their hands to have it. "About three hours of listening to some busybody shop owner asking where you got gold coin in the Queendom?"

"Closer to four, from the look of her," Michael added, letting out a frustrated noise as he fastened the button at James's waist and then started with the many buttons leading up his shirt from the bottom.

"Fuck you," Corin growled. James heard her toss the parcel down on the bed and smiled a little more brightly. At least she'd been successful in getting clothes that fit Michael in an area where *most* of the people tended toward the tall and girthy side, not the short and slight. "And double fuck you for waking me up with your nasty sex noises this morning."

"If you think that was nasty, you should have heard last time we—" Michael started and let out a small shriek as James heard the familiar sound of a fist hitting a solid point.

"Hey, hey. Don't take it out on him. He was helping me out." James reached out blindly, hoping to find her but catching only air before he heard her footsteps heading toward the door. "If you hadn't noticed, I'm kinda down on my luck right now."

"Nobody wants to hear you getting off, jackass," Corin groaned. "Anyway, Her Royal Pain in the Ass has requested your presence as soon as you're decent. I told her that might take a while, and she clarified *before noon meal*. Might wanna leave your plaything here. Sounded serious."

James muttered under his breath, knowing all too well what it was about. "No, he's coming with me. We're meeting Tyrian."

"Shit. Your kids are in town?" She sighed more deeply, and James heard the loud cry of a chair that hadn't been used in a while.

"Just him," James answered. "I think she wants me to convince him to stay here and not end up like his old man."

"Wait...wait..." Michael interjected. "*She* knows about your kids?"

"Don't take it personally. I've known James a hell of a lot longer than you have. I was practically there when that little mistake was conceived."

"Corin!" Michael growled, and James found Michael's head down around his belt and gently stroked his hair to shut him up.

"Corin has a few *problems* with me choosing to be an absent parent. I blame the fact that her mom practically shoved her on the first ship she could find after Corin turned sixteen."

"Not my fault it happened to be your bucket of shit and barbed wire," Corin said, and the chair echoed it as she stood up again. "Anyway, it's not like he even knows who you are. I mean, as far as he knows, he was probably conceived by fairies casting magic on the Queen."

"Corin." James drew a deep breath, trying not to be frustrated with her. Honestly, she had every reason to hate his choices; James sure hated them every time he considered he'd picked the life that almost killed him on a somewhat frequent basis, over being what Anika would call a *decent person.* "We'll head down as soon as we're dressed."

She didn't bother with the pleasantry of saying goodbye, and Michael didn't bother adding his opinion to the pile until he'd finished James's buttons and eased on his boots. "She kind of has a point" —he said softly and then added—"I mean, it's sort of a cruel way to put it, but you did choose to leave the life behind."

"Would you have stayed?" James asked bluntly, running his fingers through his hair in a vain attempt to make it look like less of a rat's nest. "Living some boring life with a woman you never loved, who didn't love you, playing like you actually want to be something you're not? I'm not a king. I'm not a father, and fuck knows I'm not...not that kind of guy."

Michael sighed. It was all the answer James really needed. He dressed in awkward silence, and then led James down the stairs as he was directed to the Queen's chambers by memory. The palace hadn't changed, thankfully, and James could feel the cold open spaces closing in around them even before they entered the opulent chamber that smelled of fresh-cut flowers and incense.

"I see you've brought your seeing-eye boy," Anika greeted them as Michael stopped James with a hand in the middle of his back and then guided him down onto a soft sofa. "I suppose you want him to meet Tyrian."

James braced himself, ready for her barbs well before they'd come down. He didn't want to fight, not when at the heart of it she was right. They were all right; James had always been and probably always would be a selfish bastard who chose his own way over any set before him. "Hey, you want him to know what it's like out there? Nobody knows better than Michael. He spent his whole life working for a Corporation before I liberated him."

"Liberated?" Anika chuckled. "Hearing those roughnecks you travel with talk, it sounds more like you kidnapped him."

"It's complicated." Michael stepped in, no doubt receiving an icy glare that silenced any further protest.

"Point is he knows better than I do why someone wouldn't want to join up with scavs."

She hummed low in her throat, clearly thinking over what he had said. "Fetch my son," she said to a guard James had only assumed was there. "I'll leave you two with him, but don't forget, James, I hear everything."

"Of course you do," James answered calmly. She'd always had an affinity for making herself out to be a wielder of magic in the eyes of her citizens, the Queen who hears and sees all. Truth was, nanotech cameras had been around long before the planet had people on it.

Her heels clattered along the floor, and James waited for another rebuff that didn't come. Once the doors slammed closed behind her, Michael whispered, "Do you really think this is a good idea? I mean, I don't have to be here if you're not ready."

"I'm fine. If you don't want to be here, you can wait out in the parlor." James didn't know what he really expected out of Michael; this was the first time someone he cared about had the opportunity, let alone the Queen's blessing, to meet his children. Hell, it was the first time he'd seen his son since the kid had the faculties of a well-educated child and not a barely grown boy.

Michael swallowed audibly. "No, I want to be here for you."

After a silent moment, the chance to run was snuffed out, anyway. A pair of small feet stepped gingerly through the room, barely scuffling on the tiled floor. Tyrian didn't speak, but James knew he was sizing them up the same way his mother had.

"You must be Tyrian?" Michael said, and James groped for his hand, holding fast over his knuckles to hopefully slow the impending awkwardness.

"Who are you?" a small, young voice asked. "Friend of James?"

"Yeah," James answered, flashing him a smile, wishing desperately he could see his son. "He's part of my crew, our tinkerer."

"Oh!" The boy's voice shot up. "What's wrong with your eyes?"

James didn't ask how he knew; he didn't want to know how strange it must look to him with a face that had seen the broad side of Edge's fist a couple times and unblinking eyes. "I...well, I got hurt."

"He saved my life," Michael added, squeezing James's hand. "He's a hero."

"Ain't a hero..." James replied. "A bad thing happened. I happened to be there."

"Oh." Tyrian's voice softened. A long, awkward quiet fell on the room before he asked, "Did you try disconnecting the optic nerve from the chip interface?"

James could practically feel Michael's grin spread, as he scooted forward to the edge of the sofa. "Yes! That was my first instinct, but the actual structure of the neural interface is too badly damaged. I couldn't even run the diagnostic fully."

"You'll have to replace the whole unit," Tyrian replied with an assured and confident voice that didn't belong to any ten-year-old. For James, it felt strangely uncanny, but also pretty neat. "Is the chip damaged?"

"I think so. He was hit pretty hard, and those old chips aren't as hearty as the new ones."

"You know, I'm right here," James muttered, but they seemed to have no interest in what little he could add to the conversation.

"Mom won't let me get a neural interface; she says they're dangerous."

"They are. I should know. I mean, I wrote most of the code for the last four generations of Peach chipsets."

"What?" Tyrian shrieked excitedly, and James felt the sofa dip as the boy threw himself down between them. "You work for a Corporation? That's so amazing!"

"I used to," Michael replied with a hint of sadness in his voice. "They're...they're not good, Tyrian. The Corporations, they...they're dangerous."

"Mom says that too, but you seem okay."

Michael let go of James's hand and reached around Tyrian to pat James on the thigh. "Only because James here rescued me. He made me realize that there's a world outside Corporate Space, a beautiful world."

"A boring world that thinks nanotech is going to fix everything," Tyrian shot back. "They don't think big like the Corporations do. There's so much more we could make if we put our minds to it. My tutor says one day I'll be in charge of tech development here in Verona, but who cares?"

Michael's fingers flexed and dug into James's thigh; he clearly didn't know how to answer that. Hell, James didn't even know what to say, and he usually had an answer for everything. Automatically, James answered, "I care. Hell, kid, you know more about technology than I ever will. That's pretty fucking amazing."

"James, language," Michael interjected. "What I think he's trying to say is that Verona could use someone who's not only smart, but cares about innovation. New ideas. I mean, you're only...what, nine?"

"Ten," Tyrian corrected him. "My tutor says I'll be done with my curriculum by the time I'm twelve."

"I believe them." Michael laughed, his grip letting up on James's thigh a little. "You're exactly the kind of person the corporations are *afraid of*. They don't care about new ideas, only money and power. Their people, people like me, are too blind to notice it's not even about the technology anymore."

"More blind than James?" Tyrian laughed, and James shook his head and smiled along with him.

"Hey, my blindness is gonna be fixed. Ain't a force that could fix their corruption," James grumbled, turning his head toward them. It'd be nice if there was a force that could. At least, that'd give the rest of the universe a chance.

"I'm going to fix his neural interface," Michael said, shifting away, presumably to face Tyrian. "I need to talk the guys over at the medical lab into getting the tools, so I can open him up."

"Again. Right here." James shuddered to think of going through the mess of having his enhancements done all over again.

"You need a lab?" Tyrian asked. "You don't have a lab on the ship?"

"More of a table with some bits of scrap and loose screws," Michael said. "I haven't really had a chance to fix it up yet. And the ship doesn't have the medical supplies I need either."

"Oh."

"I'm sure Anika would be more than happy to let you and her team crack open my skull. Hell, she'll probably want a video capture."

Michael laughed again, but it was Tyrian who spoke. "I can get you a lab right now if you want."

"Don't joke like that." Michael's laugh tapered off, and they realized at once Tyrian wasn't joking.

"I'm a prince. You think any of them would say no to me?"

"Well, no..." Michael started, only to be cut off.

"Prince and future head research technician," Tyrian answered bluntly. "Who's going to refuse?"

They couldn't believe it, but the kid had a point.

Fifteen: Vision

TURNS OUT, THINGS moved fast when Michael was excited and had the power of a ten-year-old prince behind him. Before James could offer much protest, he was led upstairs, three flights up, six doors down, to an unfamiliar hallway. Michael seemed suitably impressed by Tyrian's lab, and in honesty James was impressed it even existed, and some kind of genius child had been made with his paltry genetic contribution to the human race.

"Lie down." Michael said firmly, guiding James onto a table. He twisted James's head to the side to reveal his port, much to Tyrian's interest, as he began to explore the broken skin and metal with tiny little fingers. "Do I even want to know where you got those meds?"

"My tutor and I did three palm interfaces and a nanobot repair last week. I've never done a neural interface before."

"I hope I can fix the chip," Michael muttered. "Holy fuck, you've got a lot of high-end equipment."

"Language," James muttered, getting no notice. They were lost in their world of tech, and he had simply become another body on the table—not that he was entirely upset with that. "Are you sure we have to do this right now?"

"I'm heading back to Scion in the morning," Tyrian answered. "I want to see what it looks like."

James felt the sharp sting of a hypo in his shoulder, yet again, and then nothing. The room twisted and spun around him, and slowly, the excited technobabble was drowned out by that same nothingness.

It could have been hours or days, but James's bet was on the former. When he opened his eyes, James saw only blinding white pain that drove them closed again. Michael snapped to attention beside him. "James!" he called out loudly, his fingers wrapping around James's wrist, holding tight against his pulse point.

James's tongue felt like it was glued to the roof of his mouth, but his voice managed a few gravelly words. "Yeah, I'm up...I'm up...shit hurts."

"Don't open your eyes yet. I'll turn off the lights." Before Michael had even finished talking, he was up and across the room. "Okay," he called out, his fast steps echoing on the tile floor. "Open them slowly."

James didn't have the heart to tell him he'd already attempted to look into what seemed to be the surface of a blazing sun. Instead, he did as he was told. Slowly, James opened one eye and then the other, focusing on the swimming shadows above him. Then, Michael lowered the table and leaned over him. For a long moment, he was nothing but a blob of purple with blond hair and a little moonlight catching on his glasses, reflecting back at him. "Blurry," James muttered, realizing Michael was pushing a cold metal bottle into his hand.

"Drink," Michael said, not moving. "You've been out for a while; you're probably pretty thirsty." His voice held a note of excitement at the fact that while James couldn't make out anything but dimly lit blobs, he could see more than before.

The water was cold, so cold it almost burned down James's throat as he finished it. He blinked rapidly as Michael's face came into focus. "Little better now," James said, clearing his sticky throat with the last of the water. "Corin bought you a *purple* shirt?"

"Beggars can't be choosers," Michael answered, a laugh on the edge of his voice. "You have something against a little color?"

"Nah." James smiled reflexively as the lines became crisper, and he focused on soft blue eyes behind glasses. They were rimmed with red, wetness clinging to his cheeks. "Looks good on you."

Michael laughed and then drew away to sit on the opposite side of the table. "I haven't slept," he admitted with a soft sigh. "Been waiting for you to wake up for a while now."

"Tyrian?" James turned his head to look for him, and the room spun again, driving his eyes closed once more until he could regain his bearings.

"He left this morning, James. You've been out for a long time." Michael's fingers found James's wrist again, squeezing tightly. "Almost forty hours."

"Forty?" He groaned, trying to do the math in his head. It didn't seem right. "What happened?"

"You tried to wake up while I was working on attaching the chip. We had to dose you again, something stronger."

James sighed, far too tired to actually consider another attempt at moving, but managed his eyes open again. His sight was clear this time, moonlight streaming in through an open window the only source of illumination. Michael looked exhausted, and yet almost like the sort of being of purity you only read about in storybooks. "Did it go okay?"

"Can you see me?"

James looked him over as best as he could manage. A bloodstained smock was halved at his waist where his tightly balled hands were shaking. "Yeah. Looks like you had a rough time."

Michael nodded slowly and then pushed his glasses up the bridge of his nose. He looked at James with an entirely too serious expression. "It wasn't just broken, James. It was failing well before you got punched in the face."

"Failing?"

"Tech is, well, you know... It's not the heartiest thing in the world." Michael sighed and leaned forward, his glasses once more shifting down his narrow nose. "There was a lot of old damage, and your chip was incompatible with the ports Tyrian had on hand."

"So I don't have a chip anymore?" James tried to focus, tried to hear the hum of data that was menacingly silent.

Michael licked his lips, and James could see the tension written across his face. "Not exactly."

There couldn't have been another answer; chips were hard to come by outside of Corporate Space, and the ones they could get were usually outdated and probably damaged. "You used the chip from my pocket, didn't you?"

"I had to. It was the closest thing we had to a stable chip." Michael sighed again, refusing to look James in the eye. "I haven't rebooted the system yet, so your HUD is offline. I'm working on rewriting the whole code system. I can do this, James... *Give me time.*"

James tried to hold up a hand to him, but his arms refused to move. Instead, he said, "Hey, look at me." He waited until Michael looked up and then added, "It's okay.

I trust you. I mean, hell, you and my ten-year-old kid were arm-deep in my brain. You think I don't trust you to make sure it's safe?"

The corners of his mouth twitched, but Michael didn't smile. Instead, he offered a sullen apology. "I'm sorry. I wish there was any other way to do it, but..." He shook his head. "For the record, nobody was actually in your brain but me. I haven't done an installation myself in years, but Tyrian had diagrams and everything. That kid's a genius."

"He has access to all the best in life; didn't have to learn it the hard way like I did." James took pride in knowing that much, really. Anika, for all her faults as whatever a wife should be—James never really did bother figuring that one out once he realized he didn't want one— she was a hell of a mother. Hell of a ruler, too, given the general prosperity of her people.

"I wish I was that gifted at his age." Michael chuckled dryly, his fingers slipping down to clasp James's cold hand. "Of course, I probably would have ended up a lot worse off in the long run."

"I don't know, worse off than being my personal fix-it guy after getting banged around too much? Pretty sure you had it better back in the Corporate world."

"Don't." Michael shook his head and took off his glasses and rubbed the bridge of his nose for a long moment. "You know I didn't."

James thought about the scar lurking under the long purple sleeve that had only been rolled once at his wrists. He thought about the way Michael had jumped at telling him what he wanted. "Yeah," James answered. "Guess you're right."

TURNS OUT, PROGRAMMING took a lot more than James imagined, at least, in terms of time. For the better part of a week, he worked with Corin, trying to figure out a plan to get close enough to take out Lyra without half the damn scavs and mercs in the galaxy finding out who did it. Michael worked up in their room at his small datapad poring over lines of letters and numbers James couldn't even start making sense of.

While Michael's endeavor at least seemed to make headway, the crew's plan was nothing short of reckless when James presented it to Edge and Razor. Sure, they were all keen on doing what had to be done, but none of them wanted an even bigger price tag on their heads, or worse. They were discussing it almost civilly, when Anika joined them at the table.

"I'm not going back to prison." Razor slammed her fists against the table and then gestured at James with a keen-bladed knife. "None of us are going to prison for this crazy plan you cooked up."

"Nobody is going to *prison!*" James argued, throwing his hands up. It wasn't the first time she'd threatened him with cutlery, and he was pretty sure it wouldn't be the last. "I can't go in alone. There'll be too many guards to deal with on my own. All I'm asking is that you back me up!"

"I'll back you up," Edge grumbled, mouth full of greasy sausage that dripped down to his stained shirt. "Razor, just...chill. All right?"

"No," Corin said. "No, Edge. Your idea of a stealth job is only *one* explosion."

"You only need one." Edge bristled.

James turned toward Anika, acknowledging her presence, and wasn't really shocked when she remained silent. When Corin and Edge's argument got even more heated, James slammed his fist on the table to get their attention. "Look, okay, we all agree here. Lyra has to go. The best way to do that without our certain death is to have a *small* team go in, strike, and run. Razor, I know you have your reasons for not wanting to go in. I don't blame you—hell, *I don't want to go*—but the fact is you and me are the only ones who can pull this off. We need Corin in the ship and Edge riding gunner if shit does hit the fan."

Razor frowned deeper, but Anika spoke, "What about your boy, the technician?"

"Michael?" His name crawled into James's throat as an unexpected whine. "No. He's—he's not a fighter. He can't do this kind of thing."

"Did you even try asking him?" Razor shot back, dramatically looking around. "I see you haven't bothered inviting him to this little roundtable."

"It's out of the question!" James realized too late he was shouting her down and had to force back his anger at the mere suggestion Michael would be anywhere near danger.

"We'll need him to disable the systems," Corin interrupted, brushing back her hair before sinking once more into her chair and regarding her supper. "He'll handle all the remote stuff. James can force doors and, in a pinch, hack a system."

She had a point, a better one than James did, at least. James looked back to Razor. "See, you're the only choice. I need you."

"She's not the only choice," Anika said coolly, stepping up beside James's seat. "And I agree Michael should be here."

James closed his eyes and rubbed a palm over his face. As much as he'd enjoyed resting up and healing some wounds since landing in Verona, it came with the price of the Queen looming over his shoulder at every turn. "And what do you suggest, Your Highness?"

She glared at James and then sighed. "I can lend you a few of my men—unofficially, mind you."

"And in return, you get?" He left the question open, waiting for her to lay down the true price of putting her soldiers in the mix.

"Control," she stated as though it was the simplest thing in the world. "I've had visions, James, visions of a complete overhaul of the underground system, where there aren't petty warlords and benefactors like Lyra running the show."

"Of course," Razor muttered under her breath. "You'd be the new strong figurehead."

"Not only." Anika turned her attention to Razor, her gaze likely to burn holes through patchwork leather armor. "Someone has to be the alpha jackal. It may as well be someone with the worker's best interests at heart."

"Their best interests or your coffers?" Razor didn't bother looking up from her untouched plate. "There's a lot of money in rough trade these days."

"Lot of people willing to put a bullet in you too," Edge added with a throaty grunt.

James said, "I'm not giving you that kind of power, Anika. I don't care about your *vision* of what we do. You've never liked scavs for more than what they can do for you. You turn a blind eye because it keeps the peace in Verona; you're no warlord."

"It doesn't matter who ends up on top the pile if we can't take her down," Corin answered, sinking lower into her chair. James wasn't sure how she ended up being the beacon of sanity in the discussion of her own mother's murder, but he was pretty glad it wasn't all on him to talk some sense into the others. "If we don't get your tech fixed, this whole plan is a wash."

"Michael's on it," James answered quickly, glad to have the conversation turned from something other than Anika's place in the world. "He said he had to start over with the original code; it takes time."

A long silence fell over the table; even Anika stood waiting for someone to say it. Finally, it was Razor who got to play the bad guy as usual. She said, "Do you actually trust him, James? I mean really, he's Peach. How do you know you can even count on a thing he says?"

"I just know. He's *not* Peach anymore. He's one of us." There was no way James could explain to them what he was there—that Michael had been nothing more than a prisoner after he'd tried to opt out. It wasn't his place, let alone his conversation to have. He hoped his conviction was enough. "I trust him with my life."

"After he damn near got you killed..." Edge snorted.

"That wasn't Michael's doing," Corin said. "That was Lyra; she was angry that she didn't get her way."

"She didn't get her way because James prioritized his dick over money." Razor looked to James then, her eyes narrowing.

A knot of frustration curled in James's gut, and he spat back. "What would you do if she offered you a payout for your brother's life?"

Razor pushed up out of her seat, going for James's throat, but was stopped by Edge's tight grasp holding her back by the wrist. "It's not the same! We're blood."

"Like it or not," Edge said firmly, pulling his sister back into her chair, "Captain's said he's one of us. I ain't gonna fight that."

Razor huffed but didn't answer him.

"As much fun as this little family spat is, I need an answer," Anika said. "James, you need help, and I'm offering it. Same terms as always, I scratch your back and you, proverbially of course, scratch mine."

James knew the terms of her usual offers, and the sort of things that could happen when one is indebted to "the Queen." He never wanted to take that on again. "No," James answered, hearing a sigh out of Razor, echoed by Corin. "We're doing this alone. On our terms. I don't care if I have to go in myself. I'm not owing you shit."

Sixteen: If I Die

THE CODE WAS done. Michael woke James in the early hours of the morning, shoving his pad in James's face with barely stifled joy. "Wake up, wake up! I finished it! It works! My simulation works!"

James opened one eye, staring up at Michael's bleary form as it was replaced by a screen full of orange numbers and letters that didn't make a damn lick of sense. "Good, get some fucking sleep," James muttered, closing his eye again. "We'll test it out in the morning."

Michael let out a frustrated sigh, and James realized right away he wasn't going back to sleep. Hell, Michael'd probably been up all night trying to sort it out.

"Fine," James relented. "But I'm not opening my eyes while you mess around in there."

"Thank you," Michael answered, his voice pitching up with excitement. James felt the pull of tape on his skin as Michael peeled back the bandage covering the healing tissue where the old port had been removed and replaced. "The scarring actually doesn't look like it'll be too bad. You'll still be gorgeous."

"Remind me to thank my surgeon," James huffed, letting a small smile slip.

Michael didn't answer save for the slide of a jack probing into the port behind James's ear with a hollow click when it set in place. "I'm going to install the code first, then run a deep diagnostic, and then reboot. Got it?"

"Do I need to get it?"

"Not really." Michael's weight shifted, settling in beside James. He heard the low whirr of Michael's pad doing its thing. "I like telling you what I'm doing. You know, in case you're ever curious."

"Tech stuff I have absolutely no hope of understanding." James opened his eyes again, blearily looking up at him and realizing Michael had been watching his face with those soft, soulful eyes that made him feel things he'd not felt in a very long time. "I'm lucky to have you."

"Seriously? If it wasn't for me, you wouldn't need this. You'd probably be off making a bunch of money ripping off some Corporation assholes instead of planning an assassination while I try to fix my fuckups." Michael's gaze shifted back to the computer, and he pushed a few buttons.

"Not what I meant," James answered in all honesty.

Michael's eyes darted back to James's face, and he blushed around the edges of his wrinkled shirt collar. Michael reached into his pocket and withdrew another tool he then held between his lips with the tip of his tongue. Best James could figure, he was waiting for the diagnostic to finish, hopeful, given the electric current zapper thing in his hand. "Yeah..." he said without looking away from the screen. "I guess I'm pretty lucky too, for a guy who was kidnapped, wanted, and shot in the chest all in the same week." The corner of his mouth tugged, the barest semblance of a smile.

"Life's like that, right? Never know when you'll end up hating someone so much you love them." The word *love* hung in the room for a long moment, and James held his breath until Michael laughed and glanced back to him.

"Wouldn't know, never really lived before this."

James wanted to kiss him, to hold him, and hug him close for the moment, but the moment was broken by a series of loud beeps from the pad. "That good?"

"Great." Michael exhaled loudly, grinning ear to ear. "Diagnostic looks good. You ready for lights out?"

"You make it sound like you're not giving me a dose of brain damage." James laughed, knowing full well what he was getting himself into. "Joking. Joking, Michael. Yes. Please, go ahead."

James was starting to get used to the heat of the current pressed against his skin and the dark-red mark it left behind for a couple days afterward like some kind of tech-nerd hickey. Michael forced the shutdown, and again, everything went dark. Then the flashing of numbers, letters, and images flooded James's mind as his HUD powered up. The noise was back, the constant stream of upper brain chatter that had been silent for far too long. Seeing it flash and start rapidly scanning the familiar surroundings as soon as he opened his eyes was comforting. "I see it. It's back! It's fucking back...you...fucking genius!" James grabbed him then, pulling Michael down on top of him, despite the crush of his pad and the cable between them. "You did it!"

Michael laughed with him and then kissed him. For the first time since Lyra boarded his ship, James believed things were gonna be okay. "My goodness...I..." Michael stammered, flushing bright red as he tried his best to avoid James's healing wounds with his tender touches. "I'm so glad that worked."

"Of course it did," James answered, threading his fingers through Michael's hair before kissing him again, and then again. "You're amazing. It's... I can see things I couldn't see before." James focused on him, reflexively pulling up his ident card and seeing how much more depth the new code gave him. It had information about projects Michael had worked on, classified stuff that had only been marked black before. And then the flashing red flat at the very top. "You're...shit...wait. Something's not right."

Michael stiffened on top of him and then pushed away, staring down at James as though he could see into his eyes to what he was looking at.

James closed his eyes, focusing on the text below the flag. "Kill on sight," he mumbled, his throat dry. "Michael...they don't want to take you back or put you in prison." There was more, but he couldn't bring himself to say it out loud. The names of four mercenaries were listed as contracted. At the very bottom was one that made his blood run cold.

Corin DuBois.

It didn't make any sense. Corin was a pilot, not a mercenary. She always made a point of not stooping to that level like her mother's men. "I figured as much," Michael answered, but James barely heard his response over the blood pounding in his ears. "We knew something like this was going to happen, James. We'll find a way. I mean, half your crew has a bounty on their head. It's not like I'm the first."

"Yeah," James answered, letting the HUD drop to look at him, seeing the fine, tired lines creasing his eyes. "Get some rest, okay? I have some stuff I need to take care of if we're shipping out tonight."

"So soon? I thought we might stay a few more days." Michael reclined onto his side, withdrawing the jack and pushing it aside with his tools.

James shook his head, forcing his hands not to tremble as he made it up and out of bed. "If we stay much longer, bad things are gonna happen. We gotta move."

JAMES FOUND CORIN in the garden that surrounded Anika's palace. She was simply sitting, enjoying the light drizzle that came down in small bursts. "Were you going to tell me eventually?" he asked before she even seemed to notice he was there. "Or were you going to make it look like an accident?"

She looked at James and then looked down at the muddy soil under her boots. "What? You get hit in the face again or something?"

"Your mother taught you how to lie pretty good. I didn't see this coming, not from you." James could hear the blood pounding in his ears and resisted the urge to reach for the ElectroPistol under his duster.

"Don't you dare talk to me like that, James." She looked up to him again, familiar hardness in her eyes. "You don't have the right to talk to me like that."

"That's how I talk to bounty-hunting scumbags," James spat, and then bit down into his lower lip to stop himself from shouting. It wouldn't do to have guards on them, and they certainly would be, if he said some of the things on his mind.

She chuckled, a dry sound in the back of her throat, and shook her head. "I'm not a hunter."

All bets were off. James could almost understand her being opportunistic; nobody on the crew was exactly the honest type, and hell, if he hadn't told her enough lies for it to be outright hypocrisy to not understand why she would take the contract, but he just couldn't handle the innocent smile on her face, knowing what she had signed on to do. "Funny. That's not what I heard. Seems you're named on a contract for the life of someone I thought you were starting to care about."

Her back stiffened, and Corin looked up toward the cloudy afternoon sky. "I don't have to explain myself to you."

"Might help, since I'm ready to shoot you where you stand."

"Really? After all we've been through? All the years, all the blood between us, and you're so hung up on this Peach *scum* you'd kill me over it?"

"He's not like them. You know that. You've seen him; you've seen the way he really is." James stepped toward her and brushed back the thick leather of his coat, hand resting on the grip of his weapon. He couldn't bring himself to draw it, not yet, but the chances he would have to were rising every second.

"I've seen what he wanted me to see. And I saw the price on his head, James. He might have you wrapped around his scrawny little fingers, but you're the only one who's blind here. One Peach technician and we'll never have to scrape again. I know you think you're *above* living the good life, but the rest of us kinda like knowing where our next meal's coming from."

"It's not right, Corin. This isn't *you*. You're better than killing an innocent, and you know it." James was scrambling, trying to find any way out that didn't involve running in the middle of the night and leaving behind the only family he'd known for so many years.

Corin didn't answer right away, but it was hard to tell if she was actually considering James's plea. She glanced back down at the ground, and then to James, her eyes narrowing, looking him over as though she could read anything but desperation in his voice. "It was going to be quick. Painless. While you were taking out Lyra. We'd be alone on the ship, and I could say he hurt me, and nobody would know."

James sighed, his fingers flexing tighter on the grip and squeezing it hard enough to shake. "That's cold. Maybe you are your mother's daughter."

The shift of her body telegraphed her intentions clearly as she stepped forward and swung at James with a wide punch. He shifted to the side and caught her wrist. "You don't know me," she growled. "After all these years, you still only see your stupid little life. We're all stuck in this, James. How selfish are you that you can't see beyond your dick?"

"You don't get it, do you?" James shouted back at her, resisting the urge to push her away. She'd only come back at him; he knew all too well Corin was never one to give up. "You asked back in the medical center if I loved him. You know what I should have said?"

"It doesn't matter. Don't you see? I know you love him, okay? I'm not stupid. We *all* know. I'm saying some things are worth a little loss. You'll live, but how long do you think it'll be before we see any more money? Let alone enough to make sure we aren't scraping by out there. If you kill Lyra, it'll only make things that much worse...no bosses means no work, no work means SIO is dead in the water, and that blood is on your hands, James."

"We'll find a way. We always find a way."

"No, *you* always find a way. Another way to keep us one step ahead of dying out there. *I found a better way, James.* Just because you don't like it doesn't mean it's not the right thing to do." She pushed against his solid chest, digging her fist into the knot of his healing wound hard enough to feel it split open again. When James let go to clutch his side, she swung again and caught him in the jaw with another punch. "He's not worth it."

"So, so what? Now I know, and you know I'm not going to let it happen... What am I supposed to do? Leave you behind?"

She frowned and spit in James's face, backing down. "You don't have the balls to kill me. You don't even have the balls to kill *Lyra* on your own, after everything she's done. You have to drag little 'Miss Psychopath' Razor into it with you as backup."

James's hands shook, even as he grasped at the pain searing through his side. She wasn't wrong. Without recourse, not even realizing he'd had no idea what he was going to do, even when he was looking for her, James turned his back and heard the telltale click-whir of an ElectroPistol warming up. "So you're gonna shoot me in the back? That who you are now?"

"Didn't give me much choice," she responded.

Another voice came from the entrance to the garden, shaking and confused. Michael said firmly, "There's always a choice."

"You!" Corin screamed, and James whirled around in time to see her aim at Michael's chest. "You had to let him find out about the bounty. Why can't you just fucking die?"

"Don't do this!" James shouted back, reaching out, grasping her wrist, and guiding the shot up in the air as she pulled the trigger. A single blast of white-hot current hurtled into the air and came crashing back down in front of them, fizzling into the wet earth. "We'll go, okay? Me and him. You'll never have to worry about keeping the ship going again."

Her elbow slammed down, once more catching at the center of James's bandage and tearing the newly healed skin painfully. "Get the hell out of here, James. I'm not gonna give you another chance."

James didn't think—he ran. He grabbed Michael's arm at the shoulder and didn't turn back until they'd made it well past the palace gates and into the streets of Verona. He could hear Michael drawing ragged breaths beside him, so James threaded their fingers together, guiding him toward one of the few safe places he knew would be around after so long away.

Seventeen: Drifting

THE CLICK HAD been renamed a dozen times since its inception years before James ever came to the Queendom, back when Anika's mother ran the show. It had a new name again, but the same guard at the door, the same faces of haggard mercs and scavs milling around tables that had seen better days, and the same hulking gray-faced figure slinging drinks and food behind the bar. Nobody asked why they were out of breath when they dropped onto barstools, though Michael got a side-eyed glance when his face landed on the bar, flushed and out of breath.

"Gonna...have...to...shape...better..." Michael panted as Bremmel shoved a cold water bottle into his hand.

"I try to make a habit of not having to run so much," James answered, looking up at the Dalian who gave them a sturdy nod before setting down another bottle. "Pretty sure she was going to kill one or both of us. I pissed her off pretty bad."

Michael shook his head and drew several deep breaths, washing them down with water before looking to James. In a hushed breath, he asked, "What the hell happened back there? What was that about?"

James didn't answer him. Instead, he made signs to Bremmel, basic cant every half-witted scav in the trade picked up to communicate across languages, asking for privacy. Bremmel dropped a key on the bar at his elbow and muttered, "Number five, no killing." James only nodded in response and fished a gold coin out of his pocket for his trouble. It was more than he asked for, but he wasn't exactly in the mood to haggle for scraps to come with it.

Michael waited until they were safely tucked behind a locked door before again asking, "Why do I get the impression you've almost been killed a few times? What the hell happened?"

"More often since I met you." James groaned, sinking into a soft sofa provided in the lounge. It was clearly not meant for sleeping, just the sort of backroom dealings places that catered to scavs tended to draw. "Worth it, by the way."

"I don't know about that. I mean, Corin? She was so nice to me." Michael sank beside James on the lounge and took off his glasses, then wiped the sweat from them with the tails of his shirt. "What did I do?"

"There's three more bounty hunters after you too." James hated to tell him, didn't want him scared, but sometimes scared was for the best. "Your bounty's been doubled. Clear half million. More than most folks out here see in two lifetimes."

"So it was about money?" Michael's voice sounded small, like a child, and James reached for him, instinctively, to hold him. Michael's hands rested at James's sides, and then one came up bloody, James's wound already soaking through the gauze after the scramble.

James pulled away and leaned back to get a better look. The wound didn't hurt so much with the rush of adrenaline in his system, or at least, not nearly as much as the look on Michael's face made him ache. "I'll tell you a little secret about life out here; it's always about the money."

Michael frowned and then put his glasses back on, and then reached for James's shirt, tugging at the buttons. "Doesn't seem like a good way to run things."

James knew Michael had a point, but he didn't know what it was like out on the fringe either. Even in the time he'd been spent with the crew, he didn't really *know* what it was like. "You ever been stranded halfway between a couple of moons in the middle of nowhere with no fuel and no way to get any?" James mirrored Michael's frown and halfheartedly batted his hands away. "Out here, money is the difference between life and death. You think we all live like Anika? Walled up in some fucking *palace*? Do you think I married her because I loved her?"

"No," Michael answered forcefully, tugging up James's shirt, where the saturated gauze clung to his skin, despite James's attempts to wave him off. "I know you struggle. I just... I thought she liked me."

"If she didn't, she wouldn't have given us a head start." Giving in, James let Michael check his wounds before looking around the room, presumably for a med kit.

"Yeah, well...hell of a head start. You left everything behind. No supplies, no tools, no *fucking ship*."

Of course, Michael had another very good point, but it wasn't exactly like they'd had a chance to consider their next step. "That's why I'm going back," James answered without thinking. "You're staying here. She might not kill me if I'm alone."

"You don't know that." Michael pushed his glasses up the bridge of his nose with a bloodied finger before letting James's shirt back down with a frustrated sigh. "And it's not like we can pilot the ship with two people."

"Done it before." James had done it on his own, when he'd had to. Back when the SIO had barely made it into the atmo without feeling like the whole damn thing was going to fall apart, he had been the one figuring out the helm. "But no, no. The SIO is too easy to find. Too expensive to keep fueled. I'll find a jumper or something for us. People here will help."

"People here? You mean the angry-looking thugs out there, who seemed like they'd sooner cave my skull in than talk to me?"

"I said they'd help, not that they're good people. Some of 'em are, some ain't." James pushed up, letting out a pained grunt he couldn't restrain.

Michael sighed, again apparently resigned to the fact James was going. "Do you have to go to the palace? I mean, all that stuff can be replaced."

"Not all of it. But no, I don't have to go." There was another option; there usually was, but it meant owing a favor James would rather not have hanging over his head.

"Don't." Michael looked up at James then, soft blue eyes behind scratched glasses. Michael knew James couldn't refuse that look, and damn, if he didn't do it on purpose. "Please."

James sighed, reclined back against the arm of the chair, and then fished the cable from his coat pocket. "Can I use short-wave communication? Or was that fucked off in the upgrade?"

Michael nodded slowly. "It should work fine."

"Then I guess it's settled. I'll ask for *her* help."

JAMES WAITED SEVERAL hours before stepping out to the booth in the corner of the bar, slipping Bremmel his last coin on hand to have some food sent to the lounge.

After a quiet break, he contacted Anika and begged her not to ask questions, to get the things on the short list he rattled off and meet him somewhere far away from the palace and farther away from the Click. She picked a heavily wooded area on the outskirts of the Queendom, sending James on foot for several kilometers before finding her camp. She was alone, save for her usual pair of heavily armed guards, thankfully.

"How much trouble are you in?" Anika asked, glaring at James from fifty paces.

"Enough," James answered, not daring another step forward as he looked at the pack on the ground in front of her.

"Your crew, they're looking for you." She crossed her arms over her chest. "Corin says you're a traitor."

James sighed, not really in the mood to explain any of it, least of all when he was already exhausted and bloody with a hell of a walk back to where they'd be crashing for the night. "Yeah, well, she kind of tried to kill my boyfriend, so I think we're pretty square."

"I see." Anika looked down at the pack, and then back to James. "I didn't tell anyone I was meeting you."

Automatically, James replied, "Thank you. I owe you for this."

"You do." She kicked the pack toward James, and he winced, hearing the scrape and jostle inside and hoping nothing was broken in the process. "And you know what I'm going to ask for in return for this kindness."

"Believe me, this hasn't changed my plans to kill Lyra. It makes things a little harder given her *daughter* knows I'm going to do it." The thought hadn't left James's mind since they'd fled. What if she was working with Lyra now? What if she had been all along? It was hard to know anymore. "Tell Razor to take good care of SIO for me."

"You're abandoning your ship? I thought you'd die in that pile of prayers and twine."

There wasn't really much choice in the matter, and James knew it. A big ship meant being seen, especially when the person looking for them knew it inside and out. "Traveling light now."

Anika watched James for a long moment, smiling when she heard the hiss of his breath catching as he picked up the bag and shouldered it. Eventually, she said, "You're a fucking mess, James. Running again like a goddamned coward."

"Maybe I am." James couldn't bring himself to look her in the eye, not when everything she was saying was true. He was a mess, literally and figuratively, and nothing was right save for the one person he had to protect. "But I'm alive."

"For how long? Who'll cut you down first? Lyra? Your crew? Corporate Police?"

"I don't fucking know!" he spat back at her, and then sighed again, forcing himself to look at her cold eyes and downturned lips. "Doesn't really matter, does it?"

Anika laughed, a small trickling sound that sent ice through James's veins once more. "No. I guess not. Not as long as you have one more day, right? That's what you love...the never-ending threat hanging over your head."

James didn't answer. There wasn't anything left to say, and she didn't follow him when he turned and headed back toward the outer town.

When James got back and let himself into the small meeting room, Michael was stretched across the sofa with his head on one end and his knees crooked over the other. His glasses were folded on his chest with half a bottle of water tucked under his arm as he slept. For the first time since James had opened his blind eyes to see Michael's face, he was relieved. Michael didn't need to see him hurt, to watch him clean his opened wounds and try to pretend he wasn't mourning the loss of everything that had been his life before.

Like it or not, that life was over now—James was a captain without a ship or a crew. He was another fucking scav drifter like so many other wastes of flesh who walked about like men. He was nothing but the man he chose to be.

Eighteen: Looking Up

THE PAIR LEFT the Click at dawn. James managed to secure passage on a transport ship to an independent moon, off the books, and two more cheap tickets anywhere else, with one of his better-known aliases, in a vain attempt to cover their tracks should Corin come looking. She wouldn't, he knew—she would wait for them to move on Lyra; it would be the sensible move to make.

Michael didn't talk to James. He checked over the clean bandages James had put on the night before and then double-checked when they were safely stowed in the cargo hold of the outgoing ship, pointedly making no comment one way or the other. It made sense, James figured; he was angry at the situation, at what he probably felt was betrayal, and probably even mad at James for telling him the straight-out truth of the matter. It was what it was; they were on their own now.

After the first refueling stop, several hours away from Verona, Michael breathed a deep sigh and looked to where James sat pinned between their bag and a crate of ceramics bound for somewhere far away. "So this is it, then?" he asked. "We're running?"

James shrugged, scanning over the other containers for anything that looked interesting and rather enjoying his new ability to check the contents without opening things up. "It's the safe move. Get out of the star system, find a place to settle down, and pull some gold and maybe an ally or two. Once the heat's died down, we'll deal with Lyra."

"And what about the others? The mercenaries?" Michael ran a shaky hand through his thin hair but didn't look away. "There will be more of them coming, right?"

"Probably, yeah. We'll have to deal with that as it comes."

Michael shifted uncomfortably and gave a slight nod. "Anything we can do to head it off?"

James slid across the metal floor to sit beside him. Michael allowed the contact, but shied away when James tried to put an arm around him. "Only things they care about are their money and their life."

"So, we have to kill them too?" Michael whispered, looking down into his lap.

James didn't really want to kill anyone. Even with Lyra, the urge to take her life had passed once it became a contract with Anika. "That's one way of dealing with it, but chances are Peach'd just hire more."

Michael sighed again, a small sob catching in his throat. "So no matter what, I have to die?"

"No." There was an option, an expensive and dangerous option, but an option no less. "Not really."

Michael looked up at James again, his rigid posture softening to lean into James's good side. "I don't understand."

"They only know you're alive because you've got an ident chip. We get a merc to turn that in, and you're home free." It wasn't quite as simple as it sounded; finding a surgeon trustworthy enough not to take him in themself, who could also take out the device without severing his spinal cord, was hard enough. Finding a merc willing to take the card in, without confirming the kill and providing confirmation of termination, was a whole other problem.

It could be done, and had been done a few times James knew of, but it came with a price tag.

Michael nodded slowly, absorbing the new information. "How are we going to do that? It's fused into my spine."

"Fair question." And one James didn't really have a true answer to. James stroked his fingers through Michael's hair and felt him flinch, but he didn't move away. "We'll find a way. I've got some coin left from our share of the job; we'll use that to get more. We can find a good sawbones who's done it before."

"A good surgeon who's also willing to lie to the Corporations and face possible execution for removing an ident chip?"

James shrugged with his good shoulder, jostling Michael slightly before wrapping an arm around him and drawing him closer. "I didn't say it'd be easy. It's possible."

"I worry about your optimism."

"Yeah. Me too. But, we'll make it work." James didn't add the less savory thought that came attached: *Or die trying*.

Michael didn't answer so much as whine and slide down until his knees were bent against another crate, and his head rested on James's metal leg. James combed his fingers through Michael's hair, and then over his cheeks, and waited for Michael's tears to come. He needed it; crying was one of the few ways to get fear out of his system when it was too much to wrap his mind around.

"Not going anywhere," James said, trying like hell to soothe Michael's frayed nerves as much as his own. "I'm with you now."

THE FOOD ANIKA packed didn't last long—a couple days of hearty perishables and not even a week of dry rations between them—but they made it stretch as best they could. James was thankful they at least weren't starving and parched when they made it to Lunes port exchange. The fear passed and came again and then slowly ebbed away as James pulled together what could be loosely called a plan. They had enough for lodging for a month, at least—time enough to swing a few local jobs and a small ship, long enough to prepare for what would come after.

It helped Michael to plan, James figured; he liked to know what was going on and to have his ideas heard and sometimes even implemented. It was his idea that they should pull a con, dare using his skills to offload another tinkered toy on some unsuspecting investor, and Lunes was the place to do it.

The port exchange had started out as a simple local bazaar, a place for the colony miners and craftsmen to trade their goods for what they needed. Then the merchants came, and then more merchants, until the scavs found it and took over. With the scavs, came the investors, and with them, more often than not, mercenaries and bounty hunters. They were easy enough to identify. Scavs hid their weapons; mercs didn't bother—they wore them as proudly as their scars and tattoos, showing how dangerous they were, like a walking advertisement. James scanned each of them as they passed through, waiting for the drop of his guts that would come with one working a familiar contract.

Thankfully, that didn't come. He saw some familiar faces, tattoos he had seen in passing of groups that worked for one merchant or investor or another, scarred mercs who had no stake in him or his crew. He let Michael lead; he knew best what he wanted to build, or appear to build, or however that all would end up. It was James's job to try to keep Michael safe and haggle with merchants over things he couldn't rightfully identify between "metal thing" and "tech thing" and food.

Finally, Michael seemed satisfied. He brandished a new shirt for James spread on top of a collection of various items that James assumed would eventually be something either useful or would look like something useful. Michael tugged at James's elbow and pushed up on tiptoe to whisper in his ear, "We can go now, unless you want to find more food."

"They'll have it at the hotel," James muttered back but accepted Michael's guiding tug at his elbow, and they wandered away from the buzz of the bazaar toward the north end of the port. It gave way to permanent storefronts, a temple to some God James wasn't familiar with, and homes scattered in between. At the end of the well-traveled path, through the press of bodies going either way, stood their refuge. A large hotel, one of many on Lunes, anonymous and accepting payment in coin or credit like every other vendor on the planet. No names, no scanners, no questions asked, if need be. Pay up front for a bed and a hot meal.

They retired to a well-appointed room, more comfortable than back on Terro 9 but a far cry from the palace, and Michael started creating a makeshift workbench out of the small two-seat table pushed into a dismal corner. There was time, as much as they needed here, as much as they could take before having to move on. James settled in and lay down to rest, glad for the respite after being cooped up in the cargo bay for so long.

"Are we safe here?" Michael asked, somewhat unexpectedly, as he hunched over the table with his back turned to James while he laid out pieces that would eventually become something.

James closed his eyes, letting the noise all around him settle in his head. "Safe as we can be. Lunes ain't exactly the kind of place you go to stay, but it's as close to home as a drifter's gonna get."

"Is that what we are now? Drifters?" Michael's hands faltered on a piece of metal, letting it drop down against the wood with a heavy thud.

That word was putting it a little lightly. Drifters didn't have to worry about getting caught; they didn't have goals on their mind. James's lips curled, smiling on their own volition. "You're a scav now, I guess. Gathering parts, doing odd jobs. Welcome to my world."

Michael chuckled under his breath, a strange raspy sound that James didn't really expect out of him. "Yeah. Guess I am. Things are looking up, right? I have a purpose, at least."

"Careful there with that optimism. I know how much you hate having a positive outlook on a shitty situation." Michael's posture shifted, the muscles relaxing as he laughed again. Michael was getting comfortable, and considering their situation, that was a good thing.

"Sounds like you've got me confused with the guy you kidnapped." He turned back to face James, grinning ear to ear.

"Dunno, maybe... Might have to remind me who you are again with one of those kisses."

Michael shifted toward him a little hesitantly and then took off his glasses and set them down on the table, squinting as he made his way to where James lounged on the bed. "Only a kiss?"

James knew that face, when he saw it, and was eternally glad to see it again after everything that had happened. Michael was maybe not happy—happy was a strong and fleeting thing—but content. Interested, at least, and taking off his shirt. "Well, the guy I kinda love probably wouldn't stop there."

"Kinda." Michael's voice dropped to a soft chuckle, and he sank onto the bed with James, gingerly wrapping his arm over James's good side to trail his fingers over the buttons of his bloodstained shirt. When he kissed James again, that *kinda* was pretty hard to justify. James had fallen for his fair share of guys over the years, sure, but Michael was different in every way. Michael touched him like he was afraid James was going to break, nimble fingers plucking open buttons until his lips found James's chest. James stroked his fingers through Michael's dirty-blond hair, and he sighed tenderly.

"Yeah." James returned the soft sound with a delicate laugh that barely tugged at the most recent set of stitches Michael had done under duress in the cramped cargo hold after leaving Verona. He pulled James's shirt free and let it hang open, Michael's hand lingering on James's belt when he pushed up to kiss him. Michael hesitated then, soft blue eyes watching James's face for a long moment, before he moved in close.

Kissing Michael was easy, feeling the arousal build as Michael tugged open the belt and pushed away faded denim with the same fingers that wrapped around James's cock and squeezed hard. He drank James's moan, every shift of his palm drawing him harder with the same precision he used to guide his tools, the same intensity and care seeming to flow through each movement. "James..." he groaned against kiss-bruised lips, and

James answered with the closest thing he could manage to lifting his hips into the delicious pleasure of slow and steady manipulation of his manhood. "Good?"

"Uh-huh…" The sound came out a heavy sigh that was rewarded with Michael scrambling down lower on the bed, tugging off James's boots and jeans to get at his target. James didn't dare move. Between the likelihood of hurting himself, and the chances of making Michael stop, it wasn't worth the risk. Instead, James's hands found Michael's hair and raked through the dingy strands, encouraging him to keep going.

Michael's tongue teased over the head of James's cock, drawing gently at it until his moans drowned out the sound of Michael's fingers drumming on his metal leg. Slowly, James came to associate the sound with another moan that rumbled through his weedy chest and to James's very core.

"God…Michael." James's fingers curled in the sheets. Michael let James guide him, the length of his cock pushing down Michael's throat until he gagged and then swallowed. "I want you so bad."

"How you feeling?" Michael looked up at James with dreamy eyes and a warm grin, running his tongue up the underside of his cock.

If James's whine wasn't enough indication, the eager moan that came when Michael lifted his mouth away surely must've been enough to let him know he was *just fine*. "More," James answered, grabbing Michael's shoulder and pulling him closer. "Would it be too forward to ask for you to *probe* my *port*, Mister Tech-guy?" James grinned, relishing in watching Michael blush from the roots of his hair down his cheeks and throat till even his chest was nice and pink.

"That. That was a fucking low blow." Michael laughed, one hand gripping tight on each hip as he licked his lips and simply stared over his lover.

"One of the perks of being a cyborg." James let his fingers slide from Michael's shoulders down to the hand resting tenderly against metal. "Extra innuendo."

Michael leaned over him, kissing away the double entendre before resting forehead to forehead. "I would, you know. If I had the tech."

"What're you talking about?" James murmured, wrapping his arms around Michael and feeling the tension in his lithe body as Michael fought not to put his weight down against James's chest.

"Immersion. Fully interfacing," Michael whispered then, his fingers almost shaking as he traced over the healing port behind James's ear, the finger sliding effortlessly between skin and metal. Nobody had ever touched him like that before, with outright reverence, instead of indifference, at best. Even other scavs, who usually had hardware of their own, seemed scared to touch it. "Linking together, sharing sensory data. Pretty much the most intimate thing I can imagine."

It made sense, James figured. For a guy as *into* tech as Michael was, sharing that part of James as fully as when he'd had him opened up and put the damn replacement in would be more than a little arousing. "There's still one way you can be in me." James chuckled dryly, unable to resist as he slid his hands down to draw Michael's pelvis close against his belly. "I'd really like that right about now."

"You're shameless." Michael's blush warmed, but James could already feel him pulling away to get to the coat where it'd been tossed aside and find that precious little bottle of lube. "Totally. Fucking. Shameless."

James waited until Michael was halfway across the room, wishing like hell he could turn toward him and see the look on his face when he started stroking his cock, squeezing hard enough to force up a little pearl of wetness he'd thoroughly inspired. "Shame's for law-abiding folk," James answered as Michael slid comfortably between his legs, nestling his weight between metal and flesh with that look in his eyes that made James want to do frankly horrible things to him. "And Puritans."

"Oh?" Michael teased, popping open the cap before turning his attention back to James. "What's that make me?"

Reaching for Michael, once more finding that softness of his hair under his palm, James replied, "Corporate scum." His smile stretched while Michael's fade away until he added, "In recovery."

Michael leaned into James again and brushed a kiss on an old knife wound across the left side of his chest, his lips lingering on the scar before he looked up with a smirk. "Yeah, definitely hate you a little..."

Cutting him off, James managed to prop up one leg and offered a wry grin. "Hard to believe that. Almost as hard as you are right now." Michael tentatively brushed his fingers along his crack, suddenly showing the barest hint of shyness as he looked down at his naked skin. The quiet processes running in James's higher brain could see Michael's heartbeat pulsing harder as the tip of his fingertips rubbed the slickness over his opening. "Still feels good."

"Yeah." Michael flushed darker and lowered his eyes to focus on the task as small fingers were replaced by the familiar tip of his cock nudging James open slowly. "Good."

"Not gonna break me," James muttered, stroking himself with a deliberately mirrored slowness. "And even if you did, it'd be a hell of a way to go."

A moan caught in Michael's throat, and his face flushed even hotter as he brushed his cheek along James's belly. He filled James with a steady stroke of his hips, leaning over him to once more press his lips against a nest of wiry chest hair. "You're healing," Michael grunted, closing his eyes until James removed his glasses and set them on the other side of the bed. When he looked back up at James again, his hips began to shift in steady rhythm, drawing out the pleasure in ripples over his battered body.

James crested before Michael did, the painful stitch in his side barely dulling the sensation as his hips lifted and wetness slicked the top of his hand. Michael's hips slowed then, and James realized Michael was watching him, squinting at him with a broad grin. "Come on now," James said, mirroring his smile. "You know you wanna."

Michael let out a rasp of a laugh and shook his head. He lowered his eyes as a tremor ran through him, clearly riding close to the edge. His mouth opened as though he might respond; instead, a soft pleasured groan escaped his throat as his hips stopped midstroke. James felt the wetness rubbing against his skin, Michael's shaking hands guiding the head of his cock against the cleft of James's thigh.

"There ya go." James reached for him then, the tug of pain rippling through his side but not dissuading him from guiding Michael closer to curl against the good side, one arm protectively stretched across James's chest.

"Don't hurt yourself, James," Michael muttered against his ear, teeth catching James's earlobe with an unexpected nip. "Can't tend your wounds tomorrow if I'm going to be inventing."

Nineteen: In Motion

MICHAEL'S TINKERING TOOK a few days, but in all honesty, it was some much-needed time to heal and get a clearer head about the next step. Michael wanted to stay in Lunes, and didn't so much say it as extol the virtues of the kind of place where someone could eke out a living by knowing a little about tech. It was a fair enough theory, but with a bounty on his head, Michael couldn't risk staying too long in a place where bounty hunters, mercs, and scavs congregated regularly. It was an exchange, a port to change over credits and gold as much as to refuel and resupply for another long run. Every possible problem in the outer planets would pass through at one point or another, a good many of them looking for someone who knew tech. Guys like Michael were easy enough to spot: soft-handed and small, not even built like the outworlders who were bred to survive a less hospitable planet or moon than what they had in the domed, climate-controlled facilities of Corporate Space where everything was more or less handed to them for nothing more than working some cushy manufacturing or research job all day.

Michael's invention, however, was the sort of thing that Corporations wouldn't give a damn about. It was really a small autofeed mechanism that swapped out the battery of an ElectroPistol, doubling its capacity before charging from three shots to six. It wouldn't work for

James's overclocked zapper but fetched a solid ten thousand gold out in the bazaar, a ten grand that, with the five they had left, picked them up a shuttle that would easily break atmo and make it out a few planets to a relatively safe location.

It wasn't until they were well on their way to the next stop that Michael spoke about the situation at hand. "So, we're running?" he asked, staring down at the foreign controls under his hands in the copilot seat.

James didn't answer for a long moment. In fairness, they kind of were. There wasn't a good move to be had the way things were going. Just the two of them, with James on the mend even, didn't stand a chance against Lyra, and hiding him from Peach for too long wasn't gonna happen. James answered, "Consider it a strategic relocation. We've got enough fuel to make it to Autremonde, where there'll be enough people to scrape together some gold, but we'll have less chance of running into bounty hunters. They don't usually mess around with that place unless they get a tipoff."

Michael made a small noncommittal noise that started a knot in James's gut that wouldn't let go. He didn't have a response, so James busied himself with showing Michael the ropes of running copilot, watching with thinly veiled amusement as he took to the pattern with ease. "This isn't so hard." Michael beamed at him. "I could probably fly this thing myself."

"I told you." James leaned against him, forcing himself not to laugh. "If I can manage, I'm sure a genius like you could too."

"I'm not a genius," Michael replied, reaching out to grab James's elbow and squeeze it tight. "I mean, I was middle management for ages. I've never really had to think like I do out here. This is all new and amazing, and I can't believe I can actually do it."

"I believe it." James warmed, feeling himself soften in the light of Michael's surprise. "You've risen pretty damn well to the occasion, given how much shit you've had thrown at you."

Michael shrugged and leaned back in the seat, looking away from James and out at the shadows and light playing across the blackness of space. "It's so big out here." He murmured wistfully and then added, "I feel so small."

Part of James wanted to hold his tongue and let Michael have his moment, but the rest of him acted much faster. "In fairness, you're *tiny*. I mean, my son's almost your size..."

Michael sighed. "Point taken. Still, don't you ever feel like you're insignificant compared to this vastness?"

Truth was, James had never really thought about it. He'd lived out in the space between the outer planets almost his whole life. For short stretches, sure, he'd settled here or there but never for too long before getting himself skyward again. "We're part of that, though. Right? I mean, sure this is a tiny little planet hopper, but we're out here spitting in the face of ancient history that said mankind would never colonize the outer planets."

Michael nodded, and quiet came over them until James guided him through the simple task of lowering the small ship onto the surface outside the only real city on the tiny moon that was Autremonde. Lights in the distance caught their attention well before the ship's com crackled to life and their passage into the city was approved. It was a joke; really, any ship was welcome to dock. Apparently they felt the need to remind all comers they practiced execution as opposed to jailing, which may as well be the longest method of torture and summary execution.

"They kill people here?" Michael leaned closer, whispering as if they could hear him, without intentionally broadcasting to the towers marking the only entrance to the walled city. "That's barbaric."

"They kill people everywhere, man." James shook his head, offering him a tender smile. "Here, at least they tell you up front about it."

For a moment, Michael didn't speak. Then he closed his eyes behind his thin spectacles and sighed. "Is it really that bad? I mean, you joke about people trying to kill us...but it can't be that bad, right?"

Michael was in denial, and James understood. He hadn't grown up on the seemingly endless number of outer ring planets, hadn't known what it was like to live in a world of famine and drought, where people did what they had to do to survive right up to, and including, murder. Corporate Space was a life of ease, but also servitude. They'd given up freedom for security generations ago when the human race had split between the ones who played it safe and everyone else. Sure, some of the Corporate families had chosen to leave after things started to get questionable in Corporate Space, but most hadn't even seen it as an option, no matter how tight the noose around their neck got.

"You have that look," Michael muttered, drawing James out of his own foggy thoughts. "Far away. What aren't you telling me?"

"It is what it is. Sometimes you get shot or cut; sometimes people die. Don't matter if you did something or not." James shrugged and then turned away from Michael; he couldn't keep watching the pained, worried look on his face. "What matters is staying alive and doing what you need to do. If you're lucky, you can stand to look at yourself at the end of the day. If you ain't, the last blood on your hands is your own."

"Guess you're lucky," Michael said after a length of silence. James felt Michael's hand on his wrist but didn't turn back to him. "You're one of the good ones."

James didn't have the heart to remind him of the things he'd done, stories he'd already told him and the ones he never told a soul. Instead, he pushed up out of the pilot seat and bent low to exit the tiny cockpit and head out for the city.

"YOU'VE BEEN HERE before?" Michael asked, following close at James's heels as they moved through the city's narrow streets, following the signs away from the main drag.

"It's been a while. Usually SIO stops off here to fuel up or drop cargo before heading to the exchange." Michael stopped in his stride for a moment and stared at James blankly, then shook his head and let them continue toward their hopeful destination. James had friends here, well, a friend, at least, who hopefully wouldn't see only coin in their arrival. "What?"

Michael shook his head again. After a long moment, he said, "Every time I think I'm starting to understand your world, I realize I don't have a clue."

James shrugged. It was endearing, really, and kind of nice to be in the presence of someone who didn't automatically make assumptions about his life, and when he did, they were so outlandish he could chalk it up to what the Corporate bubbleheads told their kids to make them feel safe at night from the boogeymen of the outer ring. "Guess it makes up for the fact that I'm such an idiot, right?"

Michael laughed, and James felt a hand on his elbow, comforting, but not without its worry. The outer planets didn't much care who someone was or who they took home at night, but once they knew there was an attachment to someone, that person became another form of leverage. James didn't brush it aside. His pace slowed when he heard Michael's breathing become as labored as his own, the stitching holding his healing wound together giving an ache of protest with all the walking. "Where are we going?" Michael finally asked.

The place James was looking for wasn't much farther down the quiet stretch of road, a seedy little tavern on the edge of town where the prospectors and farmers gathered to play cards and drink piss water that pretended to be beer. "Not far. Keep up." James flashed Michael a grin, a little relieved when he returned it and caught up to James's long strides with his own short, quick paces. Autremonde wasn't really an easy place to get lost, consisting mostly of flat land and squat little houses beside various shops and tradesmen. They thinned out toward the edge of town, where the tight stones of the road gave way to packed earth worn down with boots and cart tracks.

The Day's Rest already showed a thin plume of smoke drifting lazily from a wide chimney in the stillness of the late afternoon, the scent of meat cooking, stale drink, and sweat seeping out through the wooden panels and old sheet-metal door. James shucked off his holster and duster, smiling again when Michael reached out to take it, and then gave James a confused look when he only hung them up on one of the many pegs by the door. Seeing his weapon tucked in neatly between rakes and old-world shotguns was a little strange, clearly. "Place is friendly," James said simply, letting his hand rest on Michael's shoulder a long moment, daring to rub a streak of road dust off his cheek with the back of his hand.

Without warning, a familiar voice piped up. "Goddamn it, Marks. Just lost a handful of gold bettin' you'd be dead before you'd show your face in here again."

James's smile twitched, spreading unexpectedly, and he looked up at a man he hadn't seen in over a decade. Dirty brown hair hung in twisted curls past his shoulders; a neatly trimmed beard was new but not shocking. "Ben." James reached out to him, approaching the bar to receive a firm handshake. "Wasn't sure you'd be around these days."

Ben shrugged, a coy smile lighting on his cheeks. "You kidding? Bought the place out a few years back, practically a fixture now. You leavin' me here was the best thing that could've happened to me."

James looked to Michael in time to see his eyebrow cocked, his glasses in one hand as he wiped them on his dirty shirt. "Michael, this is Ben. Best gun I ever saw."

"Not so much these days." Ben offered his hand, chuckling out loud when Michael faltered before shaking it, the gesture long since lost in Corporate Space. "Hung up my guns ages ago. Was a farmer for a while, but it wasn't really for me."

"I imagine it wouldn't be." James guided Michael to a stool with a hand in the center of his back, taking the one beside him. Setting a pair of coins on the sticky bar, James added, "Couple of something that'll get us really drunk for cheap. If I'm not staggering upstairs tonight, I'll be sorely disappointed."

"Wouldn't hear of it." Ben knocked the coins back toward James with a wide sweep of his hand. "Plenty of room up at my place; sure the gang'll be interested in meeting the man who broke my heart."

James shifted awkwardly, looking down at where Michael's knee had come to rest against his. "Yeah...well, those were different times."

Ben poured out a pair of thick, syrupy cups and watched them for a long moment before saying, "Ahh. New man. Got it."

"It's uh...it's complicated." Michael laughed nervously.

"Always is when you fly with James Marks." Ben offered him a wink. "Tell you what—manage those down and head out to the stitcher down the way for a clean set of clothes. I'll talk to the gang, and in a couple hours we'll set you up at the farmhouse."

"And what's the catch?" James grinned, sipping off the edge of the cup to taste a fruity sweetness tinged with strong alcohol on his tongue.

Michael fell silent again, tilting his head up to watch Ben as closely as James watched him. Ben answered, "You're going to tell me why Lyra's looking for you."

Twenty: The Gang

JAMES DIDN'T QUESTION Ben's request or how he knew. It made sense she'd tap anyone James might go to, and Ben Fisher wasn't exactly a hard man to find. They drank into the afternoon until the giddy buzzing in Michael's head had him fitfully giggling, and then succeeded in fetching fresh clothes that hopefully would come with some sort of bath at Ben's home.

James wasn't wrong. Ben left the tavern in the care of a young gray-skinned man and walked them a half kilometer toward sunset, where they saw a large farmhouse on a plot of land that seemed to be growing grain and trees with plump purple fruits. He ushered them to a back bedroom with a fireplace and put a kettle on to wash up. "I suppose I owe you an explanation," James said, stripping off his shirt to see Ben's eyes dart down to the bloody bandage on his side. "Lyra's men shot me. Well, him actually." James gestured to where Michael sat awkwardly on the edge of the bed, fiddling with the pack he'd insisted on carrying from the ship, before fishing out a protein bar.

"Don't you dare eat that." Ben offered a warm smile, peeking over at Michael as he peeled off James's bandage. "How screwed are you this time?"

"We're going to kill her," Michael answered, looking down at the wrapped square in his hands.

"That big of a mess, huh?" Ben replied. "You know she's looking for you then, at least."

"Oh yeah," James answered, drawing a hissing breath when Ben's fingers touched the heated skin around his healing wound. "Lyra, not to mention Corporate Police and any bounty hunter who doesn't care I'm attached to him."

"Shit." Ben shook his head. "Your crew?"

"Corin tried to claim the bounty." James focused on Michael, seeing him wince at the mention before he drew out their dwindling medical supplies. "Razor and Edge were loyal last I saw, but they're all that's left, and they're back in Verona."

"No kidding? You went home?"

"We almost died. I could have died," Michael answered quietly, pressing the kit into Ben's hands and letting him take the lead. "They saved me."

Ben opened his mouth to speak but was interrupted by a high-pitched squeal and the bang of the front door. "Papa! I saw you! No hiding, Papa!"

Ben rolled his eyes and James muttered, "Papa? You settled down, old man?"

"In the back bedroom, darling!" Ben called back, shaking his head. "A lot of things have changed, James. We're not all cut out for the rough life."

A small girl ran into the room, trailing ribbons behind her paisley skirt, and wrapped herself around Ben's legs. "You brought friends."

"I did, Lacey. I'm gonna clean up this wound. Can you get Momma and the patch kit?"

"Noooo!" she answered with a high-pitched giggle. "Momma's cookin' supper. I'll get it!"

"Bring her, please?" Ben reiterated, looking at the girl with a steely glare. "Daddy too."

"Fine." She sighed, an all-suffering sound, despite her grin, and then ran off as quickly as she'd come.

"Don't you start in on me," Ben said sternly, no doubt reading the laugh James was holding back. "She's my princess, and if you start in, you're out the door."

"I didn't say anything." James grinned down at Ben, wincing again when he poked at the wound.

Momma was the first to arrive, carrying an unexpectedly large medical kit. "Ben, you bringing in the trash again?" she grumbled, regarding James with a deep frown as she pushed Ben aside to tend to the wounds.

"Meg, this is James Marks. My old *captain* from back when I was scavving."

"Promise we're on best behavior, ma'am." James added, groaning when she started hurriedly cleaning the wound.

"Ain't changed at all, I see. Getting shot at, probably for stealing something," she muttered as she worked.

"He was protecting me," Michael answered, drawn out of his shy silence. "He saved my life."

It was the next voice that drew James's attention, despite Michael's sweet words. A man in the hall said, "Go play outside, Lacey. I'll call you for supper."

"Aww, Daddy!"

He didn't answer. Instead, he came in and closed the door behind him to address them directly. Well, not so much *them* as Michael. "Peach ain't welcome here. I know who you are; don't go actin' like you belong here."

"David," Ben said firmly. "Hear them out, please. For me?"

David crossed his arms, glowering at Michael from behind a pair of spectacles tucked into his bushy brown curls. "He's in Peach R&D. Either a spy or a fugitive."

"The latter," Michael shot back, pushing up on his feet and clearly taking the glare for the fear it was. "Peach ruined my life, and chances are they'll kill me."

It wasn't James's fight, but David's certainty and assumptions drew at him. "How would you even know? I mean, yeah all right. He don't exactly look like a scav, but what makes you think he's Peach?"

Ben and Meg drew in a deep breath in unison, and her fingers faltered on James's wound, scraping it hard with a swipe of rubbing alcohol. "Sore subject..." Ben muttered under his breath.

David yanked back his sleeve hard and fast, revealing raw metal and wires leading down to his elbow to show off a prosthetic mechanical hand, and a pretty bad hack job, at that. "First thing I built after leaving that vile pit. Ten years in the robotics department. They said I asked too many questions."

"Davey, that was years ago..." Meg said, returning her attention back to her task.

"Nobody leaves Peach," Michael said firmly, staring at David's arm. "Not alive."

Ben held up his hands and said, "Enough, okay? They need a place to lie low for a couple days, and then they're gone. No Peach. No problems."

It was Meg who drew the room's attention. "We'll talk tonight," she said firmly. "David, put that thing away. Nobody wants to look at your damn arm."

"I'd love to, actually," Michael piped up, and then sat back down. "I mean, later maybe?"

"Out!" Meg demanded. "Husbands out. The stew's nearly finished; take care of it."

Ben frowned, and then offered James a weak shrug before taking David's elbow and escorting him out of the room. Once the door had closed behind him, Meg added, "Don't you go filling my head with nonsense either. Ben might think you're the most amazing thing to see, but we've got a good life here. A quiet life. No messing about with scavs or police or goddamn bounty hunters." She looked up at James with a glare that frankly put Anika's calm ire to shame. "And I swear on my mother's good name, if you go changing that, I'll gut you and your Peach friend here without blinking an eye. Got it?"

"Got it," James answered quickly, the only real sane option, considering she had another pad of alcohol on his side and a really fresh entry point if she wanted it.

"Good. Now I'm gonna finish this, and then you two get cleaned up for a civilized supper, all right?"

Michael answered, before James could, "Thank you. I appreciate your kindness."

"Ain't nothing kind about it. You're friends of Ben, and that's good enough for a meal and a clean bed. Just don't go expecting more."

DINNER PASSED IN relative comfort. For his part, Michael looked thrilled to have a hot meal with somewhat familiar vegetables and meat he could identify, not to mention David's gracious answering of his questions about the arm and how he did it. Michael appeared to be careful by not asking why the limb was severed. Either that, or he knew something James didn't and kept it to himself.

"Now'days I mostly work here at the farm, but sometimes folks'll come out from the exchange, looking for someone who does tech work, with a smaller chance of stabbing, but mostly I stick around here." David sighed wistfully and smiled for the first time since they'd met him, tiny but clear as day, as Lacey cleared tin bowls and bread crusts. "It's nice. No bosses, 'cept Meg and Lacey, of course, and no scraping by either."

Michael nodded, chewing another piece of warm bread dipped in savory oil. "Did it work? Cutting it off?"

Ben moved to interject, only to have David's hand come to rest on his wrist and stop his objection. "You running, boy? Is that why you're out here?"

Michael nodded again, this time slower, his eyes glancing first toward James and then down at the plank of a table. "Nobody quits Peach. I tried to leave a long time ago, and I ended up in a Corporate dormitory."

"You quit and they made you management?" Meg piped up with a bitter laugh. "Sounds about right."

"No." David stared intently down at where Michael seemed to shrink in his seat. "It's not a promotion, not really. Management never leaves the facility—they get more credits and a place to live, but they lose their freedom. Executive security always watching through their cameras, reading every beat of your heart from the bug they put in your spine."

"I cut out the one in my arm," Michael admitted, looking down at where the brown sleeve of his new shirt covered the telltale scar. "They caught me."

Ben groaned and got up from the table, gesturing for James to join him. When James shook his head, Ben shrugged and left for the kitchen again on his own.

After a long moment, David spoke. "The tracking only works short range, maybe a few kilometers or so; it's meant to find you inside the dome." He glanced down to where his arm had been severed right below the elbow. "I wanted to make sure they didn't find me before I got out. I was...crazy."

Michael's soft laugh sounded relieved, but wary. "Theoretically, the biosign indicator has infinite range. If we had mine surgically removed, they'd still know I was alive when it happened."

"That's a big if, son." David leaned forward, his gaze only intensifying on Michael. "Even if you could find a surgeon good enough to do the job, the chances of finding a secure location that's sterile are pretty much zero."

"Surgeon ain't a problem," James interjected. "Hell, he performed brain surgery on me with a ten-year-old."

Michael shot back, "I replaced a damaged neural port I practically designed. And that kid's a genius."

"To answer your question," David said firmly, once more catching Michael's eyes, "yes. They'd know you were alive until it was disconnected from your spinal column. Guessin' that's kind of a problem when they want you dead."

"They won't stop looking for me."

"You know too much." David sighed again, louder. Ben made his way back to the table, and then deposited a warm glass of beer in front of all but Meg, who sipped her water calmly. He took a long drink of his beer before adding, "Guess we could always kill you."

Michael sat bolt upright, staring at David. "Temporarily, of course," Ben added loudly. "Massive hurt on you, enough to make the tech think you're bleedin' out somewhere."

"Stop his heart," Meg said in the same determined, yet calm, voice she'd had while cleaning James's wound. "Right before you take out the bug and then jolt it back while he's being stitched back up."

"Nooo...no...no...definitely fucking no." James pushed up out of his chair, knocking it back from the table before downing the warm, familiar beer in a long swallow. "Not gonna happen. Too risky."

"Sit your ass down, James." Ben's hard olive eyes stared back at James.

Honestly, part of him was looking for someone to talk him out of the pit of fear in his gut. James wasn't ready to lose Michael, not now, and not when things had come to such a strong head so fast. Not when James was pretty sure he'd fallen in love with him.

"It's an option," Michael said, grasping James's hand and pulling until he righted his chair and sat back beside him. "I think Lyra needs to be our priority."

"You're my priority," James muttered under his breath, flushing around the ears when Ben and Meg let out an "aww" in unison. "Corporate Police is pretty much hands-off; they're relying on the bounty hunters. As long as we can stay off the grid, we've got all the time we need to deal with Lyra."

"She's getting close." Ben set his beer down with a loud bang of heavy glass on wood. "Maybe 'bout a week ago, her men showed up here, and I haven't even seen your ass in what...twelve years? Thirteen? Got word you were spotted over at the exchange and started searching out from there. You two aren't exactly hard to miss, 'specially with your face looking like you lost a fight with the bar."

"Who is this Lyra person, anyway?" Meg asked, shooting James a confused look before turning her attention to Ben. "I always got the impression she was just someone you did a few jobs for back in the day, but this this sounds like an organization."

"She's a benefactor," James answered, honestly. "More money, connections, and influence than any of us'll ever see in our whole life. She's the link between scavs and buyers. We find what they want, and she takes a cut before paying us for it."

"She's a jackal." Ben frowned deeply. "Kind of bastard that'd sooner gut a man than pay up. Ripped us off in every deal we had with her for *damages* of all the stupid horseshit."

James said, "In her defense, I kind of screwed her on this deal. Tried to pass off a fake and actually got paid for it."

Michael added, "And she wanted me. Well, what I know."

"No shit. Head full of Peach secrets is worth a fortune," David grumbled into his beer. "So, you fucked up. Both of you. And now you're gonna what, run? How long you think you'll make it in hiding?"

"Long enough," James answered, his voice a little tenser than intended. He was pretty sure David wanted a fight. "SIO's gone. Left her back on Verona with my crew. We're down to two men in a shuttle—pretty low profile."

"And when you try to take a job, it'll get back to Lyra in two breaths." Ben's eyes narrowed. "You ain't got the honest life in you, James. Only thing you know is scav work."

"I can make money," Michael muttered, clearing his throat after a sip of beer. "I can fix damn near any tech ever created, programming, tinkering, and if I had a proper shop, I'm sure I could make enough to get us through."

"Yeah, and you could always put a great big *shoot me* target on your face." David shook his head. "There's a reason I'm a farmer now, Michael. You start calling attention to yourself, and history has a way of coming out of the woodwork. Maybe not for a few years, hell, maybe not until you're weathered and old, but eventually it's going to catch up to you if a Corporation is looking for you."

An oppressive silence fell over the table. Nobody had really said anything that hadn't already crossed James's mind, but hearing it out in the open from decent folk made it all the more clear and real. Meg broke the quiet with a final word. "It's late. You boys can stay in the back room a couple days, but then you best be moving on. Don't wanna know where you're going, but won't tell where you been."

David nodded and then Ben, who said, "It's a tough situation, but you'll get out of it. Might have to get your hands dirty, but seems like between the two of you there's enough brains and balls to sort it out."

Twenty-One: Trust

SUNRISE ON AUTREMONDE warmed across James's bare chest, drawing him to a shallow waking brought to full fruition with the sensation of Michael's small fingers caressing him. They danced around the fresh gauze from the night before and then trailed down to James's navel before rising back up again. "You're up early," James muttered, not even opening his eyes.

"Thinking," Michael answered. "Things aren't looking so good for us, are they? I mean, I know what Ben said last night, but David…the way he looked at me. I don't know if that was hate or pity."

James forced one eye open, catching the glint of sunlight off Michael's spectacles before closing it again. "Ain't good. But, we've gotta work with what we've got, right? He don't hate you, just—I don't know. Protecting his own, I think. Wary. Man's got a family to look out for; hell, I'd feel the same if some stranger showed up bringing a whole lot of danger to my doorstep."

Michael sighed, and then his fingers stilled. He flattened his palm against James's chest, letting it rise and fall with his shallow breaths. After a long moment, Michael said, "You're healing up well. If we can wait a couple more weeks, you'll be stronger, and we can strike against Lyra."

He wasn't wrong. James had hoped to have a couple weeks to spare, but the fact that she was close enough to track down people from his old crew scared him. He'd never been too worried about things that scared him—a lot of stuff did, when it came down to it, but between her wealth and general tendency to kill people who fucked her over, there really weren't many other options. "We're gonna have to be smart about it, draw her out. We can cut off her men, get her alone."

"Is that really possible?" The note of worry in Michael's voice wasn't helping.

"Probably not, but we can try." James drew a deeper breath, the stitch in his side not quite so bad as it had been the night before. "When she travels, she takes a massive ship. It's an older model, crew of at least twenty, probably more. But she never lands it, in case she has to get out of there quick. The shuttles are like our little jumper. Her and two or three guards. If we can get her down on some remote planet and take them out, maybe we can take on our own."

Michael groaned against James's ear, his glasses catching in long hair as he brushed a kiss on James's cheek. "It's a start. We'll think of something."

Thinking was about all James could do; he was trying to wrap his brain around the whole situation. Then, Michael's fingers trailed across his belly, lingering on his skin, and it was easy to not think for a moment. "Careful there. Might sound like you've got faith in me."

"I do," Michael answered without hesitation. "You know I do. Things got crazy pretty fast, but you've been in worse spots, I bet."

James couldn't think of one, but he wasn't about to tell Michael that. Not when his lips were caressing the curve of James's throat, and his body was so close. "I'm glad." James grasped for Michael's hand, holding their fingers intertwined on the slope of his belly. "I guess this is all pretty crazy, isn't it?"

"You mean the whole 'on the run' thing?" Michael chuckled under his breath, squeezing James's fingers tight. "Or this?"

"Both?" James smiled again, and then the tickle of Michael's lips on his shoulder worked toward his collarbone. Michael's weight shifted onto James's pelvis, and he leaned close with both hands planted under James's arms on the bed. "Ain't used to people counting on me."

"Your crew counted on you," Michael answered, softer than before. "You were their captain."

"They count on their own capability. They can do anything, with or without me." James forced his eyes open to see Michael looking down at him, thin blond hair spilling over the wire frame of his spectacles where it had started to grow out. "You can do anything too."

Michael blushed, the color muted against his skin where it had gone tawny with the days of sunshine so far away from the facility he'd called home. He shook his head slowly. "I can't. Not really. I don't understand this place or these people." His head lifted, and he looked toward the door, indicating their absent friends. "I guess part of me is pretty sure this is all a dream."

On impulse, James reached up and grabbed Michael's shoulder, pulling Michael down as he forced himself up through the stab of fresh pain. When James kissed him, Michael froze for only a second, and then his muscles eased as he leaned closer, accepting the gesture with a sweep of his tongue and a small sigh into James's mouth. "Does it still feel like a dream?"

Michael laughed. "More than ever. But I'm not ready to wake up yet."

The old farmhouse groaned and shuddered with a wind kicking up outside, and James could hear the laughter of the small girl somewhere far off. "We'll go tomorrow, after supper. Stop off in town for supplies and find a cave to lie low for a while longer."

Michael's gaze lowered, and he took off his glasses before laying them on the bed beside them. "Seriously?"

"Wouldn't be the first time. They're safe enough out here, and it's not like we're not armed." James reached up and brushed the hair out of Michael's eyes, tucking it behind his ear where it promptly fell back. "You can do this. We can do this. We just need a little more time."

Michael nodded and brushed another kiss across James's jaw, easing the tension with his tenderness. "Okay."

"Okay?" James's voice faltered. Michael's fingers slid down James's shoulder and then over his chest, flicking across a nipple and drawing it up hard before continuing far lower.

"I trust you." Michael's eyes flitted back upward, their blue somehow even lighter against his new complexion, a little closer to the outworlders every day. He sighed. "You've had every reason to ditch me, and you haven't."

It hurt to think about leaving him, and James assumed Michael knew why he hadn't, why he wouldn't drop Michael somewhere and run, why it mattered. "I won't," James said as firmly as a man could with a lover's hands teasing at his body. Michael didn't answer, only traced lazy circles around James's belly with those precious fingers, lighting his skin up with each touch.

After a long moment, James said the dumbest thing he could have thought of in the moment. "They teach you about the old stories in school?" Michael shook his head into James's side and brushed his lips against his skin. James continued, drawing out the moment without bothering to try to sound as smart as he actually was. "There's a story folks where I grew up told about a man who fought in the pits every day of his life. Monsters, people, anything that challenged him faced a grim death. Then one day he met an angel, a woman with fair skin and blonde hair who needed him to save her from her life of service to God. He'd fought so much he thought he could win and traveled to the Valley of Death to face the God who had created him so he might free this angel and win her love."

Michael pushed up on one elbow, looking at James with a curious gaze. "What happened?"

James shrugged. "It was a fight he couldn't win. Took on something bigger than man itself and got destroyed." In retrospect, this story was probably a bad choice.

"Oh." Michael leaned back into him then, resting his dirty hair in the crook of James's shoulder. "I guess the Corporations are kind of like a God. A real one that builds and creates and destroys."

Most outlanders would have objected to the concept of their God not being *real*, but in the course of his life, James had doubts. It was hard to see a place for God when the difference between surviving and living was the scrap of land one got run off to or had the misfortune to be born on. "I'd face God for you." The words came out of James's mouth without thought, without even considering the consequences of making that kind of commitment. It felt right.

For a long moment, Michael was unmoving. Then James felt the wetness of tears on his chest and stroked Michael's hair until he whispered, "I can't ask you to do that. I don't want you to die."

"I won't. I got something that hero didn't have…"

"A bullet hole?"

James laughed under his breath, letting the pain pull at him a little. "No, I have love. Real love, not just seein' someone pretty."

Michael sniffed and didn't say anything for long enough to kill whatever mood he'd started building. It occurred to James maybe he shouldn't have used that word; things might be moving too fast, and Michael was lost in the crazy. Finally, when James figured Michael wasn't going to say anything at all, Michael whispered, "I love you too. I think."

I think.

The words hung with James, but he wasn't going to let them hurt. Michael had a lot on his plate, and thinking about something as trivial as love when dealing with death on his doorstep wasn't exactly a priority. "We should get some more rest. I told Ben I'd help David and Meg around the house."

"Absolutely not! You're resting. If this is the last bed we're getting before jumping into the fight, you're staying in it." Michael's tender caress turned to a finger jabbing into James's good side. James grinned. Of course, he would be the overprotective type when things weren't hitting the fan so quickly they couldn't duck. "I should spend some time with David, anyway; it's nice to know I'm not the only one out here who grew up Corporate."

James laughed, and then agreed he'd at least stay in the house and try not to get in trouble. Michael's kisses stayed above the belt, but James got the impression things were all right for the time being. Maybe not great, but at least the words they'd been dancing around had been said, and they had a plan of some sort for dealing with Lyra. It was a start.

BEN CAME BACK from town in the early afternoon, dusty and dragging a cart behind his horse. Lacey and James had been playing some game he'd never heard of in the safety of their home, but she dragged James out to meet Ben as soon as she'd heard the plodding steps on broken stones. Ben raised the brim of his sweaty hat and offered them a nod, waving James away when he came to help him unload. "Leave it for now," Ben said, lifting the girl in his arms and laughing as she peppered kisses on his dirty cheeks. "Best get you inside."

James knew when things weren't right, even after the years that'd passed since he last saw him. Ben had a certain way about him when something was off. Ben carried himself differently in those moments, like he'd been spooked. James wasn't certain, though, until Ben put his daughter down and sent her out to find her mother. He regarded Ben with a drawn wariness. "What's going on?"

Ben shook his head and crossed the large central area to grab the bottle of whiskey James had left out on the table, and then poured himself a cup. "How long you been with your boy?"

James wasn't sure, really. Time seemed to jumble together when traveling, and they'd done a lot of that. "Few months. Why?"

Ben stared down at the amber liquid in the glass. "Look, David's a good guy. I trust him with my life, with my family—"

Anxiety grabbed James by the guts, and he asked, "What happened, Ben?"

Ben continued, undaunted. "When we met it was—hell, it was love at first sight. Me and Meg had been together a few years, and she loved him as much as I did."

"Ben. Come on, tell me."

Ben looked up from his cup, eyes rimmed with red James hadn't seen before. "I told David it was a bad idea. I told him your friend wouldn't make it. I'm sorry, James. You know I'm sorry."

The world dropped out from under James. He'd gotten a lot of bad news in his life and heard a lot of things he didn't want to hear, but what Ben wasn't saying was just as a bad. "You tell me right now, where's Michael? What did David do to him?"

"James—" James cut Ben off, crossing the room without pause to forcefully grab him by the collar. He shifted his weight, ignoring the stabbing pain in his side as he lifted Ben off the floor, just a little.

"Where. Is. He?" James growled, feeling the rage bubble up in him like it hadn't done in a very long time.

"You put him down now!" came Meg's loud cry as James lifted Ben even farther up. "Or, so help me, I'll put another bullet in you."

After a long moment, James did as he was told, feeling the old-fashioned rifle pointed at him well before he turned to see it. Lacey was wrapped around her mother's legs, cowering in her little blue dress, afraid of the man she'd spent the last long hours matching cards with. "Where is he?"

"We couldn't risk you knowing, James," Meg said in a calm, even drawl. "David's takin' care of him, but you can't be there."

Ben added, "It's too risky. If he dies, you'll kill David."

"He's removing the ident chip?" The realization dawned on James as hard as the lingering punch of betrayal. "I'm not killin' anyone! Where the *fuck* is Michael?"

Lacey gasped, staring up at James with wide-eyed innocence. It didn't matter. In James's mind, if Michael was lost, this whole situation was worthless. He was done; it was all over, his last hurrah.

"They're gone," Meg said, rifle leveled at James's gut. "Somewhere safe until it's done with."

"David can do this." Ben sat down heavily in his chair and downed the rest of his drink before adding, "He's got a surgeon friend in town who owes a few favors to the family—"

"You should have told me," James growled, staring Meg down and trying not to look at the scared girl hiding behind her. "I should be there with him."

"There's more." Ben's voice dropped to a near whisper as he poured another drink. "Peach is here. Town was crawlin' with security and Corporate Police. They're gonna find him, James. Him and you both." He slid the cup toward James, glass skittering across scored wood and coming to a stop right at the edge of the table. "If you don't run while you can, you're a dead man too."

"I don't— Peach? Why would they come here?" James didn't understand; most of what he'd learned about Corporate Space had come from Michael. He never figured they'd be the sort to come themselves, no matter how many bounty hunters failed to locate them.

Ben replied, "To collect their corpse."

The thought chilled him to the bone like nothing had before—the very real idea that, one way or another, the man known as Michael Bennet was dead, be it in a strictly official capacity or the real deal. James slugged the cheap whiskey and looked between them in a vain attempt to corral his anger. "Where did they go?" he asked. "I need to see him."

"If he's dead, the place'll be crawling with Corporate Police. And if he ain't, they'll be back here when they can be." Meg lowered the rifle slowly, the threat left hanging if James got out of line.

"Send the horse back when you're at your ship," Ben said, drawing a bleak look from his wife. "She'll come home. I got some provisions that'll get you on your way once it's settled."

"Settled." James snorted, slamming down the cup. Lacey jumped, and he instantly regretted the vitriol he'd held before. "You knew David was going to do this. You should have told me."

"You would have gone with Michael," Ben replied. "And if it failed, you would have done something you'd regret. I know you, James. You ain't a killer, but you don't think before you act."

James couldn't really refute that. Ben knew his past; he knew what he'd done in the heat of the moment, and he had a fair point. That said, all James could think about in this particular moment was not knowing if the guy he'd come to love was living or dead. "How would you feel?" James asked, forcing himself not to raise his voice. "How would you feel if it was David? Meg? Your goddamn daughter?"

"I'm not saying you're wrong." Ben glared up at him and then took off his hat before beating the dust off on the leg of his jeans. "It was David's call to make. I'm sure your boy went willingly. He knows what'll happen if they catch you, James. Do you have a damn clue what you got yourself into, mixing up with the Corporations? At least, with Lyra, you know she's a snake. You know what she will do to you. Those folks at Peach—those *people* are ruthless."

Meg cleared her throat loudly and laid the gun out on the table between them. "I'm gonna make some supper. Why don't you two finish this outside, then?" Lacey clung to her legs, even as she made her way to the kitchen, leaving them both behind with a lingering guilt.

"Ain't nothin' to finish, darling," Ben called back after her, receiving only a guttural sound of frustration in return. After a moment, watching James pour out the last drink of the bottle, he said, "They'll come back, James. He'll be all right, and you can deal with this Lyra situation without another gun in your back."

James didn't answer; he took his drink out to the porch and waited, watching Ben lead the horse and wagon into a sun-bleached barn before heading back to town to work the night shift. About sundown, Lacey brought him out supper and perched on his knee to "look for Papa" awhile before heading off to bed. Meg changed his bandage and muttered under her breath about how Peach better not've killed David, about how she hoped Michael was the only one they were after. James didn't blame her.

Hours after sundown, James dozed in the hard wooden chair. The moon hung high in the bright starry night, and when he heard the footsteps coming down the path, he didn't even have to squint to see them. David walked with Michael shuffling in the dirt beside him, taking slow, labored steps that sent James running out to them.

"Careful, your wound..." Michael rasped as James took on his weight, looping his arm over a shoulder.

"You look like shit" were the only words James could manage that didn't involve screaming at David for taking him, at both of them for not telling him what was going on.

David answered, "The nanobots are helping. He should be on his own two feet come morning."

"What happened? What'd you do to him?" Blood curled around the button edge of Michael's tan shirt, staining it dark with a slow bleed. His blond hair was matted against the back of his head—more blood meant more trauma. It was actually kind of surprising he was walking at all.

Michael's arm dropped off David's shoulder, and he fumbled open two middle buttons between slow, unsteady steps. "James..." When James looked at him, twin bullet holes oozed, one on each side of his sternum, bruised and burned with electricity and gunpowder. "I was dead."

"Only a little dead," David clarified. "The crack on the back of his head wasn't enough to drop him, so I shot him." It took every ounce of energy James had to focus on keeping Michael upright, and it was a good thing, or he would have probably beaten David bloody for the way he talked about this like it was no big deal. David continued, "A small incision on his spine from removing the implant, and then we had to bring him back."

"I'm all right," Michael rasped and peered up at James. He wasn't wearing his glasses, and his eyes had a dazed, glossed-over shine in the moon's brightness. "We killed 'em, James...four of 'em."

"What?" James asked, looking back to David.

David stopped when they hit the edge of the porch, helping Michael up alongside James. He answered, "Corporate Police. They came early, nabbed the surgeon before he could close Michael up, but we got out of there. I made sure he got out of there, James."

Michael coughed into his sleeve, a fine mist of blood dotting the cuff. "He didn't have to. I told him to leave me, but...he didn't. He...he gave me a gun, and I did it." Michael's voice trailed off into a soft sound, and he went limp in James's arms, a deadweight shifting into his side.

"I've got him," David said firmly, hooking his hydraulic arm under Michael's thin shoulders. "I'm sorry. I'm sorry we didn't tell you, and—" He sighed and shook his head. "—I'm sorry he had to do that. We were outnumbered." David hesitated with Michael's weight shifted uneasily between them. "He needed it."

"I don't—"

David cut him off. "He was soft, Mr. Marks. He's seen hell and back now, killed men. Made one of 'em so it'd look like him."

"I don't want to hear this." James grunted, straining with even half of Michael's light weight. "Let's get him in."

Twenty-Two: Lingering

JAMES TOOK MICHAEL to bed and patched Michael's wounds himself, and even though Meg offered, he didn't want anyone else near him or to let them see Michael's pale flesh knitting together, to feel the hot fever in his skin as his body tried like hell to repair itself.

Michael didn't wake until well after morning had come and gone, but James was beside him when he did, watching over him. James let the guilt pick at him for the man he'd twisted him into, since taking on the Rose. He wasn't like James and Ben, like Razor and Edge and even Corin. He was better than them in James's view, better than the life he'd always known.

Now Michael had blood on his hands, not to mention his only good shirt. He was changed; they all were.

Michael stirred and groaned. When James looked at him, fond blue eyes darted around and then focused on his face. Michael smiled slowly. "James…"

"Save your strength." James leaned over the edge of the bed from the hard wooden chair he'd more or less become part of. "I'm here."

Michael nodded. He closed his eyes again and then whispered, "How bad do I look?"

"Like you've been through hell." It was the honest answer, but all things said, he looked a hell of a lot better than he had when James had lain him down. James stripped off Michael's shirt and watched the new skin creeping across his chest, sewing up the gunshots and erasing the scorch marks, minute by minute. "Tech's doing its job, though."

His body shifted, and Michael let out a hollow groan, wiggling closer to him. "Hurts," he said, licking dry lips. James shot up and fetched water, only to find Michael's eyes on him again. "I'm sorry."

"Don't be sorry." James didn't want to hear him admit what had happened, especially not when his voice melted down to a rustle of his former self. "You had your reasons." James sat on the edge of the bed and helped him up enough to swallow a few sips before reclining him back against the bed. One of his pale hands rested on James's knee, holding him in place. "It's over now."

Michael sighed but didn't seem to have the strength to fight his words. James figured he'd say it *wasn't* over, that everything he went through the day before only served to make it harder for Peach to find him and easier to assume the blood he'd lost was fatal. It didn't mean they'd believe it, and definitely didn't mean that the situation with Lyra was resolved.

They napped. James napped, at least, considering Michael may as well have been dead to the world. Come suppertime, Lacey was the one who tiptoed into their room, smiling fondly when she saw Michael sitting up, working on his little tech pad, combing through lines of code that made James damn near fall asleep to even think about. "Mommy said you should come to the table," she murmured, climbing up into James's lap and wrapping a hug around his chest. "I'm sorry everyone got mad."

"Not your fault, Princess," James answered automatically, leaning into her with one shoulder, not really comfortable with the concept of kids, let alone one who seemed to take a shine to him. "It's over now."

Lacey nodded and shrank away from them, her eyes lingering on the healing open wounds on Michael's chest. "Did Papa fix him?"

"Yeah," Michael answered, pushing his somewhat bent glasses up his nose as he looked at her. "Papa helped me a lot."

Appearing pleased to hear it, the little girl let out a shrieking giggle as she ran out of the room. "Did he?" James muttered under his breath, wrapping an arm around Michael and drawing him into his chest. "Did he really, though?"

"Don't," Michael answered in the same weary voice James had come to appreciate once the rasp of death went away. "Don't hate him, James, okay? He did the right thing. I did the right thing."

James could hear the worry in his voice. Michael was mostly telling himself he did the right thing. James knew people always told themselves they did the right thing, or their hand was pushed, or they didn't have a choice. He wasn't about to break that illusion for Michael. Instead, he fished out one of Ben's shirts and helped Michael into it, rolling down the sleeves to his wrists and trying not to grin too much at how small he looked.

They didn't talk over dinner, but James could see the wary looks passing between Ben and Meg, and then there was David's blank stare. Nobody wanted to say what had to be said, so James waited until Lacey excused herself before playing the card. "We'll leave tonight," he said, even though it hurt to do so. "You've been good to us, all of you, but I know when my welcome's wore thin."

"It ain't that we don't want you here." Ben nodded, settling his fork across the tin plate midbite.

"Corporate Police might be fooled, but I don't think this Lyra is gonna stop looking, just because a piece of tech stopped working," Meg said and added, "I know it's harsh to say, but you two bring a world o' hurt with you here, and I'm not having it."

"It's fine." Michael forced out the words, his supper barely touched, save for a few bites of greens and his water. "I'm all right to travel, and you people have done a great service for me—for us." He looked up at David, who also hadn't seemed too keen on eating supper. "David, I don't know how to thank you for what you did for me."

David shook his head. "Don't thank me, boy. Stay alive out there. Don't do anything stupid."

Michael nodded slowly. "I'll try."

"I'll make sure he doesn't," James muttered into his last bite, swallowing down tough meat with a gulp. "Even if it kills me."

"Don't talk like that," Michael growled, the sound of his anger unexpected and a little unsettling in James's ear. "I won't let you."

An awkward quiet fell over the table. Ben started clearing plates, and Meg excused herself to put Lacey in bed. David only sat and stared, silently watching. He didn't move when they got up to go pack their bags, but was gone when they left.

HORSES WEREN'T EXACTLY uncommon on the outer planets, especially the closer you got to exchanges. Farther out you'd be more likely to see pack animals bred to haul and pull a plow through stony drought land, but it hadn't been more than a few years since James'd had the chance to ride. Michael curled up on the cart Ben had given them, tucking himself down between a barrel of water and a crate of supplies that'd get them through long enough to make it to the next stop. He grunted and moaned with each lurch of the horse, James's clumsy driving drawing out pain that cut through him.

James apologized, but Michael didn't answer. The rough road gave way to no road at all, cutting through the plain desert as the night's chill began to settle in. There was no way to avoid it without going through town, and knowing Corporate Police were around, James didn't much like that idea. Instead, they circled around the town, hours out of the way, and by the time they made it to the shuttle, the sun hung toward the middle of the horizon.

"Time to wake up," James said, patting the large animal's haunches after dismounting and heading toward the cart. His body ached from the long ride, but it had felt good in its own way. "How you doing?"

Michael looked back up at him from a nest of dusty blankets and rubbed his bleary eyes, waiting until he'd put his glasses back on to answer. "I've been better."

James nodded and started loading the gear into the shuttle's storage compartments, not surprised when Michael struggled to drag a crate up beside him. "Let me get this," James said, receiving a clear glare. "I know, I'm hurting too. I don't know, it makes me feel useful, I guess."

"Maybe I want to feel useful too," Michael answered curtly, letting out a soft grunt as he dropped the crate and then kicked it open to take out one of the four heavy jugs of water halfway to the shuttle. "I can do this."

"I know you can—"

Michael cut him off. "I can do a lot of things, James. You don't have to treat me like a child here! I can—I can work." He sighed loudly and wiped his rolled sleeve across his sweaty brow. His voice dropped to a cowed whine. "I can be like you."

The empty crate James had precariously balanced between his knee and the shuttle crashed down, and he didn't particularly care; he was staring at Michael and watching the frustration vent off him. After a long moment, he simply stared as Michael forced himself to take a second bottle and drag it to the ship. "You can't." He reached out and took the bottles, despite physical protest. "I mean, you can, but please don't." The wind kicked up, spinning dust between them and the ship, and James had to lower his eyes against the blowing sand. "I don't want you to be like me."

Michael didn't really answer. He turned his back against the sand, and instead of heading for the crate again, he made for the cockpit.

James continued loading alone, finishing soon after sunset without so much as a word from Michael. When he dared to approach the open door, Michael was curled up in the copilot seat with his datapad out on his lap. "Look..." James started, only to be waved off with a dismissive hand. He pressed on. "You know the reason I like you, right? You ain't like me."

"I am," Michael shot back and closed his eyes, turning the pad over as he set it aside. "You don't know what happened last night."

"You killed a man."

He nodded slowly, eyes closed, and whispered, "I killed four men."

The thought made James's guts ache, but the lines creasing Michael's exhausted face were worse. "That fucking David..."

"David lied," Michael stated simply, turning to face James when he opened his eyes again. "He didn't shoot me. They did. Two of them did, and I shot back, and it was horrible and...I...I..." He hiccupped, the sobs coming on quickly until James could see the wetness rolling down his cheeks as he forced out the words. "I didn't stop until there were no bullets left, and I was dying. I could feel myself dying, and I—I didn't want to wake up."

James sank into the pilot's seat and reached to cradle him only to have Michael pull away and trap himself against the instrument panel. "Michael—"

"All I see when I close my eyes are their faces. They had families, maybe kids. They were doing their job."

"Their job was to bring you back dead or alive, Michael. Preferably dead. You stood your ground."

"I know. I just..." He trailed off again and shook his head, then wiped away the tears with the back of his hand. "I just did my job too. How many people died because of me?"

It was something James had already thought about, and also something he'd seen in himself. "Don't matter now. You got a choice; you don't gotta do it anymore."

"But I did." Michael sniffed loudly, fighting off another soft sob. "I'll have to do it again too. David knew that; that's why he didn't say goodbye. He knows there's no happy ending for people like me."

James reached out to him again, and this time, when Michael flinched away, he cupped his hand at Michael's shoulder and pulled him back in. "I'll take care of it," James answered, his dirty thumb wiping away a stray tear. "I'll take care of you."

"No!" Michael shouted, eyes opening with a fierce gaze. "That's—that's the problem. I don't want you taking care of me. I need to learn how to do this. I need to learn how to survive out here."

The anger in Michael's eyes confused him, and James answered, "Not alone, you don't."

Michael lowered his gaze and turned his attention back to the console, already starting the ignition sequence. "You don't know that."

"I ain't going anywhere." James leaned back in the pilot's seat and crossed his arms over his chest. Michael could easily fly the damn thing, especially with the next set of coordinates already plugged in. "I know that much."

"We don't know what'll happen tomorrow. For all you know, Lyra or Peach will have men waiting for us when we land. For all we know, this ship is bugged," he answered as the shuttle hummed to life and began coasting above the dusty trail they'd followed to land as it gradually gained altitude. "This shuttle could explode any second now."

"I've been a dead man for twenty years," James huffed and then looked out at the long expanse of space that stretched out in front of them. "Been a pretty good run so far. Guess if that happens, my luck's run out."

Twenty-Three: The Calm

IT TOOK TWO days for the fuel to start running low. Two days of avoiding each other as much as two men could actively ignore each other when trapped in the same hundred square feet of shuttle.

James turned off the autonav and then looked to Michael, who was once more pouring over his datapad as though he could see the ultimate truth of life wrapped in strings of code. "You see that dark-blue moon?"

Michael looked up and pushed his glasses up the bridge of his nose. Following James's gaze, he saw their destination and nodded. "Yeah. It looks cold."

"You're going to land us right in that big glowing spot. Learned everything else under fire, may as well let you try not to kill us on impact."

Michael's eyes widened. "What is it?"

James couldn't help smiling to himself. The lone moon of Atros didn't have a name as far as he knew, but it did have the single largest city he'd ever seen. Larger than the exchange, larger than the lush expanse of Verona. "Did you ever hear stories about the pre-Corporate cities?"

"Sure. Ancient Seattle was basically Peach Corp phase one." Michael's brow creased. "It's an old-world city?"

"It tries to be. Mostly it's one of the few places the Corporations can't go, and mercs won't." Michael shifted awkwardly and then took the controls. He added, "There was one of the first prison colonies there 'bout a hundred an' fifty years ago. Started a few years before the corporations took over for criminals considered too dangerous to keep on the central planet till the corporations started sending their prisoners there. There was a revolt against the system after that, the prisoners making a sort of truce, and over the years it got bigger an' bigger. Only a few come in, but nobody leaves. Mercs ain't welcome since most of the families got put away for it, and benefactors don't bother."

"Wouldn't Lyra think you'd go there, though? Somewhere she can't operate?"

James chuckled dryly. "Hope she does. It'd save me a lot of work if the gangsters take her out."

"So we're staying there?" Michael looked up with a confused crease across his brow. "Or only getting fuel?"

"We'll figure it out after some rest." James reached out and dragged his thumb along the arm of Michael's glasses. "Don't know about you, but I kind of miss having time together when we ain't flying."

Michael didn't answer. After a long moment, the quiet buzz of the shuttle the only clear sound, he said, "Does the city have a name?"

James knew it wasn't anything either of them had really done or said that set things off-kilter between them; they both had frayed nerves, and the weight of what they had been through and what was to come hung heavy over them. The blankness of Michael's stare dug at him. "Warfield."

The process of disembarking at Warfield was far different than most places. Upon landing, their shuttle was searched and James's weapon removed to remain on the ship until departure.

"James Marks," a leather-skinned creature drawled, towering a full yard above him as they examined the pair. "Your contract work with Lyra DuBois has been terminated?"

"Yes." James shook as large, unfriendly hands examined his healing wounds, groping at his naked chest before patting down his weathered trousers. "I'm outta the game since she tried to kill me. Ain't cut out for scavving the way the benefactors are running things."

They made a brusque guttural sound that came off as disapproval. "And your purpose here?"

Michael spoke up. "We're looking for honest work."

They laughed then, a rumbling sound like a cave-in rattling through them. "A Peach Corp runaway and a disgraced scav, and you want *honest* work?"

"He's telling the truth, Kovar." A small ethereal voice came from behind them as thick metal devices were fastened around their wrists. "Though the one called Michael has removed his ident chip, no doubt with significant physical trauma, and is not eligible to work for Corporate credits." The soft voice paused a moment and then added, "They are afraid of Lyra DuBois, particularly the one called James."

"That will be enough, Car." Koval leaned in closer, and Michael shuddered under his imposing presence. "You will report to the head of Block B within ten hours for a more thorough memory scan. Until then, Warfield welcomes you."

James didn't wait for further pleasantries before grabbing his shirt and leading Michael out of the spaceport, by the hand. "Is it always like that?" Michael asked. "All those questions? A mind reader?"

James answered as they hurried out to the slight chill outside, pausing to fumble closed the bottom four buttons of his shirt. "The last time I was here it was worse. It's pretty much still a prison. The interviews keep it safe, just like the walls and sentries posted on every corner. In a lot of ways, they never left the old way of livin'."

"Sounds familiar," Michael said. "Why are we here, really?"

"According to you, we're looking for work. Nice trick, by the way. Mind readers are hard to fool."

"I wasn't fooling them, James. We need a plan. Working for a little while you finish healing and my nanobots do their job is a good plan, like it was a good plan *before* we left the exchange." Michael looked around them, examining several signs written in a script he couldn't even begin to decipher. "Where are we, even?"

James tugged at Michael's sleeve, drawing him out of the footpath they were following and into an empty alleyway. "Okay, first some ground rules. You don't admit you were ever Corporate; you don't let anyone know you have money—"

"We don't—"

"And you don't, under any circumstances, do some of the things you might see me do in the next five minutes."

"Wait, what?" Michael asked, receiving only a silent hand signal to wait before James slipped back out into the busy crowd.

James blended in, weathered equally in face and clothes, as he searched out a suitably distracted quarry with a pouch that looked weighed with gold coin. After the prison changed, the gangs took over, and the natural order of things when there was no means of production was to take control over what few resources there were with none coming in from the corporations. Over the years, James figured, they'd picked up trade and farming and with that the old gold standard above Corporate credits.

He wasn't wrong. When James fell back to where he'd left him, Michael was sitting on the ground with his back against a dirty stone wall and was reading on his datapad. Michael barely looked up to acknowledge him.

James said, "Gold is easy to come by."

"You stole it." Michael frowned.

"From someone who was probably a murderer, yeah," James answered. "Anyone who's not a kid was either put here for their crimes or, like us, is running from something. Ain't really good folk."

"Says you." Michael looked up at James as though he were about to continue. Instead he asked, "Can we find a bed somewhere?"

James nodded and then sat beside him. "I'll check my memory files. I don't think it's changed much since Razor and Edge escaped."

Michael's brow creased. "Escaped?"

"Yeah...well..." James shifted awkwardly. "The thing is...just...okay, so..."

Michael put down the pad and rested his head in his hands. "How fucked are we?"

"Honestly less fucked than before we stopped here, probably." He let out a sigh. "Most of the people here can't leave. They came here when the Corporations started using it as a dumping ground for people they didn't execute. The block leaders were put in charge of deciding who can and can't leave."

"I...I don't understand."

"We'll worry about it after some rest, okay?"

Michael looked down at his hands a long moment and nodded. "All right."

FINDING A CHEAP place to bed down and something dubious but warm to eat was enough. After filling their bellies, James took the wash kettle off the fire, crackling warmth filling the small room as curls of pale smoke escaped the single window they'd barely opened against the encroaching night chill.

Michael had begun to understand the rhythms of James's lifestyle. Without asking, he took a folded cloth from the bedside table and a chunk of dry soap. He caught James watching as he folded it into the cloth. "What?" He barely smiled, but the quirk of his lips was a relief to James after the last few days.

"Just watchin'," James answered, setting the pot on the end of the bed as Michael dipped the cloth and began to work it between small hands that had begun to callus. After a long silence, well aware of Michael's delicate movements as he washed up, James answered, "I'm sorry I didn't tell you more about this place."

Michael dragged the cloth across his bare chest and then under his arms, considering it for a long moment. "I get it. Can you tell me more?"

After stripping off his shirt, James gingerly peeled away the old dressing at his side. The wound was healing well; a couple weeks without running or getting hit would have it closed up easily. He answered with cautious optimism, "In the morning, we'll meet with the head of this sector. We won't be able to lie or anything like that, so all the cards will be on the table. After that, they'll tell us if we're free to come and go." James drew a deep breath, considering his words carefully. "If they think we're a threat, they'll keep us."

"They kept Edge and Razor?" Michael asked in a softened voice as he moved closer to James, gently taking the cloth across the broad expanse of James's shoulders.

He leaned in, surrendering himself fully under Michael's tender touch. "They kept Edge. The person he reported to felt he was a danger to the outside world."

"Oh?"

"They kept Razor when she killed that person."

Michael's hand stopped midstroke, a slight tremor betraying the calm tenor of his voice. "You helped them escape? Killers?"

"Not killers," James answered, pulling away. It took a long moment to collect his nerves and look to Michael, who had taken off his glasses and caught James's gaze with complacent and gentle eyes. "Not any more than you an' me, at least. They're blood, devoted to each other, no matter what. I'd kill for you as easily as she does for her brother."

That was enough to bring Michael around, it seemed. He drew a deep, somewhat shaky breath and then went about carefully washing James's back without further comment about killing. "Will they think we're dangerous?"

"They might. It was a risk I was willing to take for a little safety. Worst-case scenario, we end up settling down, making a life here. You could tinker like you were; I'll help. You could teach me."

Michael shifted his weight, pushing closer until his thigh aligned with James's solid metal limb. After a moment, he then swung himself over James's lap and leaned his head carefully against his lover's chest. "What if I don't want that life?" he asked into James's skin, brushing a kiss there.

"It wouldn't be bad here. Work, roof over our heads, no more running."

Michael shook his head. "I've spent my whole life a prisoner, James." He hesitated again, seeming to carefully consider his words before adding, "I want to fly."

Reaching down between them, James lifted Michael's chin. He hadn't considered Michael would ever want that life—hell, sometimes he didn't even want that kind of life. "Then we'll figure it out."

Michael nodded and then stilled when James leaned in to kiss him. "Let me clean your wound, please?"

James didn't fight him. Instead, he pulled the warm kettle closer and tried to restrain himself as Michael took great care washing away the road dust before obtaining a clean cloth and bandages to finish the job. When they finally curled up underneath a drab gray blanket, naked, despite the room's only warmth coming from a fire that had burned down to embers, he could feel Michael's heartbeat chest to chest.

"I'm sorry," Michael whispered. "For what I did."

James raked his fingers through hair that had begun to grow long, pulling it out of Michael's face before cupping his cheek. "Don't be." He leaned in and brushed a kiss on Michael's forehead, warming with the fond brush of lips against his thumb. "You're still the man I fell in love with."

Michael chuckled softly and looked up at him with a wry smirk. "Every time you say that, our love feels a little more real."

"Suppose I shouldn't say anything else, then," James murmured, wrapping his arms around Michael and pulling him in as close as he could. "Until you know it is."

Michael stroked his fingers along James's side, tenderly tracing the edges of his bandage before closing his palm over the thickness of James's hip. "Promise me, I won't wake up back at the facility, and this isn't just a dream."

James kissed him again, letting the warmth of their embrace wrap around him. After a long moment, he said, "I promise. I'm pretty sure dreams don't hurt this bad."

"A nightmare, then. It's not a nightmare?"

"I hope not," James whispered. "For both our sakes."

Twenty-Four: Turning

MICHAEL SHIVERED IN the middle of the night, thin arms clinging around James's hips as he pressed his head into James's neck in search of warmth and comfort. James drew their blanket up higher until he could only see dirty-blond hair spilling out over the top and rubbed his palms over Michael's shoulders. "Shh...it's okay, let's warm you up."

"So—" Michael whimpered into James's skin, words coming in bursts. "So cold. Why is it so fucking cold?"

"It's a moon," James answered, curling his fingers in the nape of Michael's neck. "We're on the dark side now. A few more hours left before it starts warming up."

Michael whined and tucked his knees up closer to his chest, letting out a small yelp of surprise when his shins grazed over James's metal leg. "This is terrible. I can't sleep like this."

James understood. Corporate Space was climate-controlled with no sense of hot or cold, and so far they'd really only seen the temperate side of Verona and the heat of every other damn place on the outer planets. Certain moons were a whole different experience. "Yeah, me neither." He let his touch tease at the nape of Michael's neck a while longer as the shivering began to slow to occasional jolts of chill. Then, he once more followed the lean arch of Michael's shoulder, tracing down to the hand on his hip to wrap his fingers over Michael's. "Let me warm you."

They were both aware of the friction between them, ever since Michael had technically died, and James couldn't help feeling a part of Michael really did die, when his chip was removed, and he had to do what he did. His pulse climbed as Michael shifted awkwardly against his chest, and then slowly rolled onto his back and looked up at James with a coy smile. "I don't think I've ever seen you be so subtle, James," he teased. "Half surprised you didn't grab it."

James chuckled and shook his head, before subtly brushing a kiss on Michael's cheek as he leaned in comfortably. His palm once more stroked over Michael's skin down his belly to trace over the sparse blond curls below. "I'm trying," he admitted. "I want to give you space. I know what you went through was hard."

Michael nodded. "It's done now," he whispered, lifting his pelvis to guide James's hand to wrap around the base of his cock, the flesh already responding to the much-needed touch. "I want you, James. If you still want someone like me."

Leaning the slightest bit closer, James found his lips and kissed Michael again, his large palm wrapping around Michael's partially hard cock and squeezing, stroking base to tip with the languid caress of Michael's tongue opening his lips and exploring his mouth. Breaking away with a moan, he whispered, "No. You—not someone *like* you. You're still the man I fell in love with." His fingers gripped tighter as the blength thickened against his palm despite the chill, and he rolled his thumb over the head of Michael's cock, smearing it with wet beads of arousal. "No matter what, ain't nothing gonna change that."

Michael moaned, lifting his hips as his thighs began to shake with something other than the night chill. "Promise?" he gasped, eyes half-lidded.

"Promise."

Michael pushed against James, letting out a delighted cry when James fell back and let Michael roll him off his side. "Okay…" Michael's smile widened, a shiver catching him as he covered as much of James as he could with his small body, and the blanket shifted below his shoulders. James opened his thighs wider, pulling aside the exposed metal for Michael's comfort as he began to thrust against the fold of James's fleshy thigh. "Oh…kay…"

It was James's turn to shudder, but not from the cold. Shaking fingers wrapped around his hardness and began to tug with each thrust. He gasped, watching the intent focus on Michael's face, the way his lips drew into a determined bow and limp curls fell into his face as a moonlit blush crept down his throat and shoulders. "Don't stop." He reached for Michael, drawing him close enough to feel the gentle weight against his wound shifting as he rutted even faster, wetness streaking on his skin. "I want you."

Whimpering, arching his back with each awkwardly angled push, Michael let James guide him. He let James's flesh wrap around him, holding him close as the waves of lust warmed him. "Want you…" he cried into James's solid chest, another soft mewling sound escaping his throat when James's rough hands slid down the cleft of his ass and opened him, a thick finger pressing against his hole with enough pressure to make his cock twitch eagerly. "Gonna fuck me this time, James?" he panted, flushing even warmer at the words tumbling out of his mouth and the hot implication of them. "Please?"

It wasn't his intention really, but James couldn't refuse that face, couldn't let him down. "Best way to interface, right?" He grinned wickedly. "I want to see your face when I do."

Michael let the blanket slip lower, pooling around his hips as he once more braced his hands at James's waist and sat astride his generous hips, rocking the tip of his dripping cock against James's abdomen as James's hardness prodded between his thighs. "I'll beg…" Michael murmured, leaning in to kiss James as he snatched the thin bottle from the open bag on the side table. "For you."

From anyone else that thought wouldn't do a damn thing for him, but the note in Michael's voice made James throb even harder. "Beg," he said, eyes glazing over with unfettered desire. "For me."

Kissing him again, Michael begged silently with his tongue along James's lips. His hands stroked the cool liquid over James's cock until it was warm and the hardness was angled toward its goal. "Please…" Michael whispered against his lips, unintended desperation in his voice. "Please, James? I want to feel like I did before."

There was no way to fix what had been done, no way to wash away the blood on his hands and the fear in his heart, but James knew he could at least remind Michael of the strength he held inside. "Yes," he whispered back, barely lifting his hips to have Michael's slim body take control and fit against his hips. The tightness shifted slowly around him as Michael sank down, taking it in with a hiss of held breath between his teeth. "Yes."

Leaning into James's chest as much as he dared, Michael shuddered and stifled his cries with each gentle roll of his hips, guiding himself in a slow dance of desire. Despite the chill, sweat beaded at his brow, and a pink flush colored his once-pale skin. "Thank you," he gasped, the thought punctuated with the gentle rasp of skin against skin.

Wetness spread across James's belly, thick hot pulses as Michael dug against his skin with each calculated push downward. James grasped his lover by the hips and let himself believe for a moment Michael had wrested control and it wasn't his injury that left him passively delighting in the moment. "Little harder," James grunted, eyes half-lidded as Michael kissed him again.

Michael moved against the solidness of James's body, arching only when his chest brushed against the soft gauze on James's wound, riding out the tender push of the hands on his hips. He let out a soft cry of surprise when James pushed up against him until he was sitting in James's lap and wrapping his arms around him. "James, careful…"

"This is what I imagined earlier," James breathed, rolling his hips despite the tugs of pain as he hooked his arms underneath Michael's. "Holding you in my lap like this, kissing you and loving you with my body as much as m'heart."

Michael whimpered, the angle affording little comfort when James's cock stretched him with each slow stroke. "I love you," he whispered, resting his head on James's chest once more. "You know that."

"I do," James moaned, Michael's arms clinging tighter around him as his heels spurred at James's hips. "I know." There were more words tickling at the back of his mind, but making sense of them in the small hours of the morning with Michael's mouth pressing kisses on his throat was more than he could manage. With one final push, James lifted his hips as much as he could, driving Michael down into his lap and filling him to the root. Pleasure washed over him in pulsing bursts amplified by the unintelligible words being whispered into his chest.

"Careful," Michael whispered, after a long moment had passed, and James understood those soft-spoken syllables again. "Please be careful."

Leaning down to the bed meant letting go of Michael, but reluctantly James sank back to the thick bedding and looked up at him with tenderness written across his unshaven face. "I'm careful," he muttered back, gently prodding his side along the edge of the bandage. "Promise it'll be fine when we go for our meeting."

"Will they see it?" Michael asked, rocking his hips, happily astride James's lap and enjoying the moment for what it was. "Will they know who shot you?"

James reached for him again, fingers brushing along Michael's sides down to the junction of their hips. "They will." He chuckled. "Maybe they already do. The mind reader when the ship docked...they knew."

Michael nodded slowly, shifting off James's hips with a hollow moan. He stretched out alongside James and curled his fingers on James's chest. "Should I be scared of them?"

"No," James answered, taking a long moment to rake his fingers through Michael's hair. "Put on the kettle—we should be prepared for later."

THE GRAND BLOCK hall had once been some sort of work area for the prisoners held at Warfield; at least that's how Edge had described it to James in the days after their escape. The block leaders had each claimed their stakes; block B was held there. The leader, a large man with gray skin and stringy black hair, sat at a desk on one end. Two chairs sat in front of him and an adviser at his side. The mind readers had also come with the prison, beings that few planets in the known outer realm had ever met. Nobody knew where they came from, and the few folks who ran into them knew they liked it that way. There were rumors of technology being at the root of their abilities, some Corporation experiment gone rogue, but also whisperings of magic and the occult frequently dismissed as quickly as they'd come up. Anymore, it was hard to tell if magic was ever anything but technology people didn't understand. James liked to think maybe they were something wholly special and different from anything else living.

"Michael, please sit." The reader spoke in a soft whirring of noise that seemed to form words not unlike the hum of nighttime insects. They gestured to the chairs and then folded their hands.

"Not you." The block leader looked at James with an expression James figured was somewhere near disgust. "We'll talk to the Corporate slave first."

"I'm not a slave," Michael hissed between clenched teeth, staring down the reader with obvious intent. "Not anymore."

"The slave has removed his collar." The reader tilted their head to the side as though examining a curiosity. "He is confused. Adrift."

"He's with me." James stepped forward and raked a hand through his hair. "Anything you get from him, you get from me."

A small smile, almost imperceptible, crossed the reader's slender pink lips. "This is true. One James Marks is also lost. Though, with more purpose than his partner."

"You gonna let me talk or keep running my thoughts until we're good an' tired?" James frowned, mirroring the reader's crossed arms. "I'd kind of like the comfort of a seat if we're gonna be here a while."

"You ever shut the fuck up?" a small, familiar voice called from behind them. "They were savin' the best for last."

A chill ran through James, and he shuddered visibly. "Corin. You, uh. You found us."

"Corin—" The block leader spoke, his voice sounding like the slow churn of rock against rock as he leaned back in his plush chair. "—has been waiting for your arrival. She spoke to us about the broker, about your deal."

"You cheated her," the reader said, staring down at Michael intently. "And you did so without a second thought. Without concern for your own safety, or of the people you keep ship with."

"Self-preservation," Michael answered, not turning to look back at Corin. Instead, he sank down a little lower in his chair and stared back at the reader. "She tried to kill us before she knew we cheated her."

"She shot you; you cheated her; I tried to capture your boyfriend; now here we are." Corin stepped closer on the gray cement leading up to the slab of the block leader's desk. She stopped in front of James, smiling when he turned to face her. "Reward's off the table. Story is a bunch of Peach security ended up dead out by the exchange, Michael too. Looks pretty good for a dead guy."

"He's not worth anything to you anymore, Corin. Why you comin' out here after we left Verona?" James took a step backward, not entirely sure if he was aiming to be farther from her or closer to Michael.

Corin shrugged and raised her eyes toward Michael. The reader answered for her. "She wishes to fight the tyrant called Lyra DuBois."

At the mention of her name, the block leader perked up and stirred in his chair. "Lyra? She was your benefactor."

"Was," James answered, staring Corin down. "I'm sure you understand breaking contracts over getting gut shot and all."

"They do intend to commit murder, which is a punishable offense in all regions of the outer territories," the reader said in a calm monotone. "And it would not be the first murder for any of them."

The block leader grumbled and shifted again, peering at them uncomfortably. "James Marks, would you be the one responsible for the escape of those called Edge and Razor Portillo?"

James turned toward the desk and nodded slowly. "I am. They saved my life a hundred times over. I'm only standing here right now by the good graces of my crew, including that man you got there in front of you. Now, I'm sure you already know I'm on the mend, and all I ask is a couple weeks' time to heal up before we're out of your hair."

"I'll work," Michael interjected. "Any tech you have, any tech you need—"

The block leader cut them both off. "You're planning a murder."

"That's right." Corin stepped up beside James and turned her attention back up to him. "My mother's got too much blood on her hands to be left standing. If we don't take James and Michael with me, I've got two in atmo and half an army ready to move on her, if they don't see my shuttle in ten hours."

That was all news to James. He looked back to her, concern crossing his face. "You have gotta be shitting me."

The reader spoke. "This is a lie. There are few forces prepared to move against Lyra."

Corin folded her arms across her chest and huffed. "Fine. Not exactly half an army, but we have people. With or without you and your little boyfriend, James. Hell, even without me, Lyra's gonna die."

"Quiet!" the block leader shouted, his voice the sound of boulders on limestone reverberating off the bare walls. "Li, are they murderers despite their crimes?"

A hush fell over the room, and the reader, Li, looked over them methodically. James's eyes glanced from Corin to Michael and back again, before Li answered the block leader's question. "None of them *enjoy* taking lives." Their large, pale eyes lingered on James, a small note echoing from the back of their throat. "The one called James Marks takes great pride in his skilled theft of Corporation assets, even the one that got away."

Michael chuckled in the back of his throat and glanced back to James, a soft smile creasing his lips. James answered, "Ain't no friends of the Corporations out here. Least not for long."

The block leader's black marble eyes narrowed on James, and for another long moment, silence blanketed the hall. "One week, you two." He gestured with a broad meaty finger toward Corin and James, and then to Michael. "You may come and go as you please."

"I'll go," Corin said firmly. "In a few hours."

There was no conversation, the block leader staring at Michael until he pushed up out of the chair, and they hurried out of the hall with Corin, once more seeking out the warmth of James and Michael's hotel room.

Corin was the first to speak, as James went about building a fire, settling down into the room's single chair before saying, "I ain't gonna kill you. Either of you."

"Well, you'll have to pardon my difficulty believing that," Michael piped up, wiping his glasses on a soft washcloth. "Since the last time we crossed paths you were ready to hand me over to Peach Corp."

"Last time we crossed paths, you were worth more money than I'll make in a lifetime." Corin glanced from Michael to James. "And now you know that's not a problem."

"You sure about that?" James asked, lying on the bed to take the pressure off his wound. "Corporations can be relentless; maybe they don't think he's dead."

"James—" Michael started, but Corin cut him off.

"Your boy left a hell of a mess behind him. Ben and his gang said you'd be running for a place Lyra can't find you." She frowned deeply. "Couldn't make heads or tails out of who was who down there."

"You went—" James started.

"Of course I went." Corin sighed and dropped her head into her hands. "Anika's been looking for you a couple weeks now, and once your boy dropped off the radar, she figured you'd be coming back to make a play on Lyra from there."

"And her army?" James asked.

"I'm honestly a lot more worried why you ain't curious about the mess he made." Corin lifted her chin toward Michael. "I've seen murder, but I ain't never saw anything like that."

"I..." Michael started, but finished with a soft exasperated sound.

"It's done, Corin. Ain't no sense in making him out like some kind of monster. We need to focus on the threat here."

Corin nodded and then looked down at the gulf of rough-hewn planks called flooring. After a long moment, she said, "Lyra's actively looking for you. After her goons made a little intimidation stop in Verona, Anika pledged the soldiers she could spare."

"That's great!" Michael straightened up and looked to Corin. "How many? A few hundred?"

"Twelve," Corin responded. "And a volunteer medic."

"That's good, great actually," James answered. With a laborious groan, he pushed up off his back to sit beside Michael. "But what does she want in return?"

Corin shrugged. "Ask her yourself when you come back. That bullshit is on you, *Your Highness*."

Twenty-Five: Execution

NESTLING THE SMALL shuttle into SIO's only dock was the first of many dangers James knew would come at him fast, once he left the security of Warfield, after a couple weeks of bed rest. That said, he was mostly healed and almost as restless as Michael was to get the whole ordeal finished.

The next flash of danger was Razor's pistol leveled at his head when he boarded. "Ahh. Mutiny?" he asked casually, dropping his knapsack as he raised both hands. "You'll probably want to wait until Lyra's out of the picture before killing me." He was fairly certain, despite her frequent threats, Razor never had intended to kill him. He was also well aware he'd been wrong many times before.

"Don't have to kill you." She frowned deeply, lowering the barrel down to his crotch. "Just make you suffer for taking off like you did."

"Aww..." James smirked. "Missed you too." The electronic whirr of her weapon charging was pretty much expected. "Look, what's done is done. I already wasted enough time healing. We have bigger problems."

Anika's voice spoke with sudden clarity in the cargo hold, drawing James's attention to where he'd failed to notice her standing against a large supply container marked as holding meal supplements and water. "My soldiers are ready to move. This ship made it here in two weeks; that gives you time to figure out your plan without killing each other."

"Anika." James stumbled a step forward, brushing aside Razor's weapon without a second thought. As far as he knew, she had never left Verona in her lifetime. Hell, last he'd heard, her people would surely die out if she did.

She held up a hand, stopping his advance before he made it even halfway across the holding bay. Anika said, "This is my fight, too, James. She threatened my people."

James nodded and looked to where Corin and Edge stood silently by, waiting to see what came next. "Let's get moving. Razor, Edge, if you're willing to fight, I need you to work with Michael on upgrading weapons."

"I had some great ideas for increasing the lethality—" Michael started but cut off when Edge put a large arm over his shoulders and started walking him toward the barracks.

Razor hesitated and then turned to lock eyes on James. "If my brother dies—"

"I know," James said. "If we do this together, I think none of us have to."

She stared at him a long moment and then nodded slowly. "After this is done, we're cutting our losses. Can't live like this, Captain."

James nodded agreement. "Thank you; you know...for not killing me."

For the first time in what felt like a lifetime, James saw the twitch of Razor's lips that came closer to a smile than he'd ever seen from her. She gestured for Corin and breezed past James to the cockpit, leaving him alone with Anika.

She spoke first. "I'm here to make a deal."

"Damn it, I knew—"

"You don't know shit, James." She glared up at him. "No favors, no debts hanging over all of us. Blank slate. I want your word that after Lyra falls, you'll come home."

"Anika…" He sighed and then paced to a large crate he could lean on. It occurred to him, for the first time since their daughter had been conceived, they were actually alone together. It was strange and more than a little awkward. "I—look." He drew in a deep breath; he was poised for her icy glare when he looked at her, but she only gazed back with a crease of worry across her brow. "You know I can't do that."

"I know you won't. You choose not to out of some stupid sense of needing a bigger world." She frowned, glancing down to where her immaculate high boots gently scuffed against the metal hull. "I don't want you to do it for me, not even for the Queendom."

"Then what? You never wanted me to stay before." James remained stoic, but internally felt something had changed in her, in both of them maybe. What it was dawned on him as the gentle worry knit across her face turned to obvious sadness. "Tyrian?"

She nodded. "He's not in Verona—"

"I know." James cut her off. "So, what? You think he needs his *friend* James hanging out and encouraging him not to be a scav?"

"I want you to tell him what it's really like." She lowered her head, her voice dropping barely above a whisper. "I want him to know why he doesn't have a father."

The bitterness gone from her voice rose up in James's. "Fuck you, Anika. Just. You know what? I'm done. Fuck your army. I'll handle this. I'm done."

"Don't be stupid," she hissed between clenched teeth. "Do you realize how hard it is for me to ask you for this? I want you to be in his life, James, but I'm not going to act like he'll accept your excuses as easily as I did. You owe it to him."

"Go ahead, Anika. Say it."

"What? That you owe me? Damn right you owe me. You *left*, James." She stood up, back straight as she approached him in two long strides, eye to eye. "I gave you a chance to have everything. You could have been safe, fed, not scraping by to scrap out another piece of space junk or dip into bounty hunting and pretend you won't have to do bad things; hell, maybe rip off another Corporation that's eventually gonna catch up to you and put you in prison or worse." She crossed her arms across her chest and sighed again, defeated. "It's high time I collect, wouldn't you say? Make the ledger even."

James took a step back and shook his head slowly. "I'll talk to him, but I can't stay."

Anika snorted. "After Lyra falls, someone's going to have to fill the power void. Wouldn't it make sense to be out on a neutral planet? No broker or buyer presence, people would come to you in safety."

"Are you suggesting I take her place? Have you lost your damn mind?"

Anika looked up at James, her hair falling in clean ringlets along her chubby cheeks. "I'm suggesting you change the game. Someone damn well has to."

The ship shuddered all around them as the speed picked up, no doubt Corin's way of telling them to hurry it along. James frowned and looked around the quiet bay for a reason not to answer.

"You don't have to live in the Queendom, James. Scion would take you, and fuck knows you've spent your share of time with the rabble in the Midlands," Anika said, voice softening. "Think about it, okay? I know you don't want to settle down, but I guess part of me is hoping that eventually the blood on your hands will slow you down a little."

She had a point; she usually did. James nodded slowly. "We'll see. Pretty sure Michael's just getting started with being an outlaw." He smiled at the thought. Hell, he'd go out of his way to find a duster in the smallest size.

After a quiet moment, James tilted his head toward his wife and then started walking toward his lover. "You really like this one, don't you?" Anika called to him in a voice holding a hint of humor but lacking her trademark cynicism.

"Yeah, I do. Guess I love him, after what we been through."

"I'm glad. You deserve to find what you've been looking for." Anika's heels clattered on the hull as she followed him in step.

"You implying I gave up the good life to find a man?" James chuckled, relieved it didn't come with a tug of pain anymore.

"Not really. You just seem happy now, happier than you ever were before."

A BREEZE BLEW across the barren tract of nothing, heat wrapping around them as James, Michael, and Corin hopped off the train stalled out on the track between cities. They wouldn't have long, maybe an hour's window before the train started back up again and left them out in the dust, but it was long enough.

"Ready for this?" James asked, catching Michael's elbow in his palm and pulling him close midstep. "It's not too late to back out."

Corin fell in behind them and made a show of slamming the butt of her ElectroRifle across the small of James's back, staggering him. "We're probably being watched," she hissed under her breath. "At least, act like you're about to be handed over."

Michael drew a deep breath and let it out between clenched teeth. "Yeah," he answered. "She won't come out for only you."

"Don't know that," James said. "Maybe putting a bullet in me the first time was good enough."

"He's right." Corin dug the gun into James's back when he hesitated short of their goal. "You're the cake, but he's the icing on top."

"So what if she kills us both?" James said. "I'm not worth much to her either way, and Michael's a threat."

"I'm a threat who knows things."

They stopped where the sand went from smooth taupe to a mottled chocolate brown, wetness spreading below where old roots cut through the earth and threatened to grow plants despite the inhospitable climate. "On your knees," Corin said firmly. "Michael, do you remember how to disrupt the cuffs?"

Michael tucked his arms behind his back, pulling away from James in the process, showing the small metal pin he'd tucked into his palm. "It's not exactly a complex jamming mechanism." He groaned softly when Corin grabbed his shoulder and pushed him down. "You think she'll believe you got us both?"

"She'll believe you gave yourself up when Corin took me down," James replied, dropping to his knees without further prompting, his artificial leg splayed out in its own apparent protest. Corin fastened his cuffs and tugged them tight. "Watch the ears, okay? I don't want my sight offline again."

Corin made a small sound somewhere between a sigh and a laugh. "If he doesn't come to pretty quickly, you know what to do?"

James moved to answer but shut down when Michael answered in a calculated tone. "Grab his gun and focus on Lyra. Start firing and don't stop until she does."

"I'll cover you," Corin added. "Don't worry about her goons, I only have to hold them off as long as it takes for the cavalry to show up."

In the distance, the low growl of an old motor cut through the desert stillness. "Shut up." Corin pulled up her radio to call coordinates back to Lyra's people. Without warning, after closing the communication link, she slammed the butt of her weapon hard on the back of James's head.

It could have been minutes or hours. When James came to, the smell of ozone, gunpowder, and blood hung heavy in the air. "Don't move," Lyra growled in a haggard voice, and James felt a boot pressed against the back of his neck. "You move, pretty boy, and I'll cave in the back of your skull like a melon."

James's gut sank. "Michael?" he called out with the vain hope things weren't completely fucked. "Where's Michael?"

"Aww." Lyra pushed down harder, pain washing over him. "I'm touched. Here I am ready to end your pathetic attempt on my life, and you go asking about your little boyfriend. Don't worry, my daughter made me promise I wouldn't harm a hair on his big fat head. You, well, you're a different story. She knew better than to ask for leniency after you fucked me over."

James tried to answer, a strangled croak the only sound he could produce.

"I assume you're a little confused now. See, Corin knew you'd play along with her, if she stopped going after the Peach boy. After you took the money and stepped out on your crew, my daughter was looking for stability. Someone she could trust."

The pressure on the back of his neck shifted off, and Lyra kicked James in the side before rolling him onto his back. Looking up at her, James only saw her face haloed in desert sunlight. Blood trickled down her forehead where a dark scorch mark showed off where an ElectroPistol had struck true.

"Your boy landed a good shot before my men could react. I've got to give it to him—he is one squirrely little bastard. The soldiers—they were a nice touch. I'll be sure to chastise Corin for failing to warn me about Anika's role in this pitiful little coup. Of course, I can't blame her for wanting the insurance just in case I ended up turning on her; it's what I'd do in her shoes."

"Fucking kill me," James groaned. "You want your revenge, take it."

"As much as I'd enjoy ending you right here—" Lyra groaned. "—you're more useful to me alive, and as long as I have *Michael,* you'll be a good dog and mind your manners, won—" The words ceased as a loud crack rang out in all directions across the flat landscape.

Lyra stopped then, fingers opening to drop her rifle before absently rising to the center of her blouse. Redness blossomed between her breasts across the pale-blue linen, curling slowly as she gasped for breath several times before wordlessly slumping down onto his legs.

James turned his head, not entirely sure what was happening was real, and saw Corin about a hundred yards away. She dropped her rifle and ran toward them.

"Where's Michael?" James demanded, unceremoniously lifting Lyra's body with his mechanical leg and then rolling away. "Is he alive?"

Corin gestured toward the direction they'd come from, toward the train they had hijacked to get there. Shaking, she dropped to her knees and reached out to Lyra.

For the first time, James was able to survey the damage as he picked himself up to find Michael. Three dead Verona soldiers, four of Lyra's men. The asshole who had shot them back in the cargo hold so many months before had burns across his leathery skin and a knife lodged between his eyes.

By some stroke of luck, the train hadn't left yet. The passenger car was open, and the field medic from Verona jumped down to intercept. "I need to check you out," he said firmly. "Corin said—"

James brushed him aside and climbed up. He wasn't sure what he'd expected, but the sight of Michael lying on a passenger bench, wrapped in James's duster wasn't it. "What happened?" James asked the soldier who seemed to be watching over him. "Did Corin hurt him?"

The soldier shook his head. "He wanted to go back for you after we killed Lyra's men. He took a bullet in the shoulder in the process."

With a sigh, the medic added from the doorway, "I sedated him on Corin's order. He's patched up; he'll be awake in a few hours."

James collapsed on the bench across from Michael and curled onto his side. "If she's not back in twenty minutes, leave without her."

Twenty-Six: Something is Out There

IN THE END, James made good on his end of the deal, if only to buy them both time to heal physical and mental wounds after what they'd been through. They were set up with a small house in the Midlands outside the Queendom's walls in one of the rowdier parts of the planet. It took only a few days to begin working on his promise to give Michael a workshop of his own, both in their home and on the ship housed less than ten kilometers away in their private landing bay.

It would take time to gather the trust of the people, but as Michael worked on tech from the sister cities and things that would fetch coin on the open market, James wrote out a guild charter for the first association of independent scavs in generations. He met with Anika, and more than anything, James *tried*. He wanted to believe something good was on the horizon, and he could be an agent for change.

When Tyrian was sent to them, James and Michael sat with him together in their little house about as far from the palace as possible. Water and fruit were laid out, and for a long moment, nobody said anything.

"There's a few things we should talk about." James broke the silence, pressing a cold jug of water into his son's hands.

"You two are together," Tyrian said in a voice that came off as childish mockery. He tapped his fingers in odd rhythm along the bottle's edge, not quite impatient, but noticeably acknowledging the discomfort in the room. "I figured you were, the way Michael fretted when you were under."

"Not that." Michael frowned. He pushed his glasses up higher on the bridge of his nose and added, "That's not exactly a secret."

"Tyrian." James spoke firmly. "Your mother thinks, and I guess she's right, but she thinks it's time you know your father."

Tyrian's eyes widened, and for a long moment, he stared silently at James. Then, slowly, he turned his gaze toward Michael. "Must be where I got my mind from."

James held back a laugh, a derisive snort slipping out. "No. No. You got that from Anika. Hell, I wish it was Michael. No, it's me, Tyrian. All the gifts from your father, all those visits where we talked about what I do..."

"Oh." Tyrian's mouth drew up in a small half smile, and his tapping slowed. "That's... Actually, that makes sense."

James reached out to him, but the boy ducked away with little effort. "Why didn't you tell me before?"

"She didn't want me to be in your life like that. She's a good leader, a good mom too. I'm not exactly good at much."

"He loves you," Michael added, clearly about to say more when Tyrian stood and stepped away on tiptoe.

"Can you show me the ship?" Tyrian asked. "You've told me stories about SIO but never let me see inside her."

"Sure thing," James answered, grinning widely. "Tell you what—if you help Michael get the workbench situated, I'll do a couple orbits around the planet."

The small smile creasing Tyrian's lips spread wider. "Thanks, James. I can call you that, right?"

James nodded. "I'm still your friend, I hope. And I'm your example for why you don't want to be a scav."

MICHAEL WOKE WITH a start, dragging deep breaths and shaking as a fine sheen of sweat beaded at his brow. James took his hand and squeezed tightly, eliciting a deep breath. "What is it?" He asked.

He shook his head, pausing a long moment before he answered, "It must have been a nightmare. I remember pain, and the medical office bunk, and feeling so alone."

"I'm here," James whispered, brushing a kiss on Michael's sweaty brow. "You're fine. Everything's fine."

Slowly, Michael's lips curled in the barest hint of a smile. His voice came out soft, but sure. "I dreamed about Corin. That she really did turn on us."

"She didn't." James nuzzled against him, pressing his body against Michael. "She made the right choice."

He breathed heavily. "I hoped she would. I don't know why I keep thinking about that day."

Resting his cheek on Michael's chest, James kissed the soft skin there. He was content to listen to the steady thrum of Michael's heartbeat. Then, Michael said, "How long do you think we'll stay here?"

"We're gonna stay here for a little while," he answered calmly, going over the things he needed to do yet to get the guild in motion. "I need to contact some people."

"Oh."

"I, uh, I sort of promised Anika I'd sort this out and maybe do father things too."

Michael closed his eyes and nodded slowly.

"How are you feeling?" James asked as he trailed his fingers over Michael's bare chest, hesitating where the new scar had formed on his shoulder.

Michael groaned softly, but didn't protest. "The nanotech is working, but I might always have a scar." He sighed. "I'm not used to being shot. Pretty sure that's not a thing."

James's fingers traced the warm skin surrounding the scar, carefully avoiding any spots that might be tender, and then slid up to cup the side of Michael's neck. "It's over," James murmured. "We won."

Michael was still once more, his skin barely warming to James's touch. James said, "What's wrong? Don't say *nothing* either. I know when you got something on your mind."

It took a moment, but eventually Michael answered, "I wonder what I'd be doing right now if you never came for the Rose. I mean, Lyra's kind of the whole reason we ever met, right?"

"Well..."

"And now we're free? What is that even like?"

James leaned over Michael and stopped his wondering with a gentle kiss. Breaking away, he whispered. "I never told you what SIO means, why she's called that. Stands for Something Is Out There."

Michael cracked a wry smile. "That would be SIOT."

"Shh. Don't ruin my moment." James mirrored Michael's smile and kissed him again. "The point is, now that we don't have to run, the only limit we got is our coin. And...well, I didn't want to ruin the sweet moment, but Tyrian isn't the only reason we have to stay."

"You're gonna go through with it and be a full-time guild liaison?"

"I don't know what that word means," James admitted. "Guess I'm the guild leader or whatever. I'm gonna make sure the benefactors know independent scavs like me don't have to work for them; we can do it all on our own. I've already contacted Ben, and he knows some trade folk over at the exchange willing to work directly with scavs to get contracts, even to work without contracts."

Michael's smile spread, and he reached up to pull James closer, letting out a small squeal when James rocked his hips to press ardently against his side. "Well, if you need me, I'll be where you are."

With a throaty, pleased sigh, James wrapped his fleshy leg over his lover's. "Was hoping you'd say something like that. I know you got your heart set on travel, but it'd be nice to have a place to come home to, right?"

"I have my heart set on you," Michael answered without hesitation. "I think I've had enough adventure to be satisfied at least long enough to do what you need to do here for now."

Kissing Michael was easy, tender brushes of lips leading down until James lavished affection at the junction of Michael's shoulder. Encouraging him, James felt Michael turn belly to belly with him and begin to pluck at his shirt buttons. "You sure you're okay? If you're not feeling like doing anything but bein' close, we can cuddle a good long while."

"I'm fine," Michael answered as he pushed against the solid mass of James's chest until James let himself be rolled onto his back. "I want to be with you."

"I'm with you." James helped Michael scramble on top of him, chuckling as those nimble fingers tugged at his zipper and folded down the stiff denim to get at the flesh underneath. "Wow, you ain't wasting any time, are you?"

Michael planted a hand on each of James's broad shoulders and pushed up enough to allow James to slide his jeans lower. "Want to be close. Feels like Warfield was another life."

"Because it was." James looked up at Michael, the dim natural light of late afternoon quickly going dark, and couldn't stop himself from reaching for him again, from drawing Michael close and peppering his clean face with kisses until he felt drunk. "We're free now, Michael. No more running and looking over our shoulder." He laughed, a wild sound tearing through the quiet. "And I swear to you, I am gonna build up the best damn workshop you ever had so I can watch you work."

Michael blushed and slowly relaxed into James's chest, allowing himself to be held. "It's already going pretty well; there isn't too much more I really need."

"Whatever it is, we'll get it." James smiled against the smooth skin of Michael's cheek. "You'll have to make a list. Might take a while to get everything, but you're worth so much more than a guy like me can give."

"You're enough." Michael's slender fingers stroked away the scratchy fabric of James's shirt and began to follow the crisscrossing network of white scars on his tanned skin. "Everything else is just extra."

It would be easy, James thought, to stay there and lazily comb his fingers through Michael's hair until they drifted off to sleep. It was Michael who ultimately propelled things forward. His lips found the scruff on James's jawline and kissed there tenderly as the hand that wasn't focused on balancing wrapped around the girth of James's cock and gave a firm squeeze. "We could fool around here any time, you know," Michael offered. "No neighbors, no crewmates…just the two of us out here enjoying life."

"Feels good," James grunted as delicate fingers caressed his flesh. Michael teased at his balls, playfully squeezing between slow strokes along the partially erect shaft. "Don't force yourself. I can wait if you're not feeling right."

Nuzzling into the side of James's throat, Michael made a small sound of protest between eager kisses and licks. If the sure grasp of his fingers was any indication, James figured he was fine. At least fine enough that James's toes curled against the thin blankets between them and their bed.

Gradually, Michael slid down to sandwich himself between James's side and the edge of the bed without losing the quickening pace of his strokes. "Can I—" Michael groaned, and James recognized the sensation of Michael's hardness sliding along the cleft of his thigh, where metal met flesh.

"Fuck, yeah," James groaned, brushing away the hand that stroked him to rest his palm over Michael's hardness. "I want to watch."

Michael shuddered and hid his eyes behind James's arm, flushing red in the dim light. "D-don't. Don't look at me."

"Okay," James whispered. He removed his hand, allowing Michael to take the lead. "I won't." He pressed a kiss on top of Michael's head and found the hand that wandered across his chest. "Talk to me?"

Michael shuddered. His fingers grasped James's hand, and he buried his face in James's shoulder even more ardently, tilting his chin to mutter at him. "It—it's weird, I know..."

James let out an anticipatory moan as Michael began to rock his hips deliberately, sliding his cock first along the warm metal of exposed casing and then up and across scarred skin. "It's not," he answered. "It's good."

Feeling Michael's smile on his skin, James drew his lover's fingers up behind his ear. He moved gently, allowing Michael to trace the small pits and grooves, the clean scarring where it had healed since those same hands installed the port. "Is that—" Michael started but finished with a moan as his hips began to quake with each thrust.

"Yes." James's voice dropped to a hushed groan. When he let go, Michael's fingers moved freely, caressing across metal and skin with delicate reverence. "Please."

Michael gasped as he pressed his fingertips against the port's tiny dust cover. His body shifted methodically against James, driving his cock at a comfortable angle along the jagged scarring. "James..." he whimpered and then shuddered as his short torso folded along James's side. The spasms came hard, warmth spreading across his thigh in small pulses that elicited almost pained whimpers.

James joined him then, gripping his own thick shaft and forcefully tugging base to tip in time with Michael's ragged breath. Michael groaned against his ear, "Please, fuck...you're so amazing. I love you."

The last whispered words tickled in James's ear, and a warm grin spread across his face. Life was good despite the change of pace, and he had a good man and good sex and no lurking fear he was gonna die that day.

Michael's fingers slowly stroked the port once more, teasing it as James's hips began to rock with each hard stroke. "I think once my workshop is done, I am going to fuck you until I can't move"—Michael smiled against his ear and added—"and then keep going after a long nap."

It wasn't the first time James had felt the twinge in his loins double him over as he laughed, and hopefully, it wouldn't be the last. Such dirty words out of Michael's mouth were worth the warm fluid streaking his palm with each rough push of his cock in his fist.

Drawing desperate breaths, they curled against each other. James whispered, "I love you," along Michael's sweaty hairline. "I'm so glad I found you when I went looking for something new and unexpected."

About the Author

C.A. Blocke is a thirty-something writer who's been captivated by the magic of how people relate to each other for as long as she can remember. Far more than overarching drawn-out plots, she prefers to focus heavily on relationships in various situations that feel like real life—even when at its most surreal. Real Life, she feels, is messy and complicated, and that shines through in her fiction where the road to a happy ending frequently isn't just a straight line. A long-time reader and writer of fluffy character-driven pieces, her style tends to highlight small slices of life that come together to form a whole picture of the plot.

She is a gender-nonconforming, demisexual-identified female who feels most comfortable writing unconventional relationships involving non-heterosexual couplings. Sexual identity often colors her works and features heavily in finding the comfortable place where identities can collide with minimal friction. She enjoys exploring different takes on 'acceptable' sexuality and blurring the lines between what is expected and what really happens.

A small-town Arizona native, the Southwest and its rural communities fascinate her—particularly the rigid-identity politics and the ramifications of breaking the social norm. Of course, that's not to say that she doesn't also enjoy writing about urban life and the various challenges present in the big city. While most at home writing contemporary romance with a warm little erotica twist, she's very prone to following her muse down the dark alleys and open valleys it drags her through—making it nearly impossible to know what genre will take her interest next.

Twitter: @afullmargin

Other books by this author

"A Secret Shared" within *Beneath the Layers*

Also Available from NineStar Press

Connect with NineStar Press

www.ninestarpress.com

www.facebook.com/ninestarpress

www.facebook.com/groups/NineStarNiche

www.twitter.com/ninestarpress

www.tumblr.com/blog/ninestarpress